CRAVEN'S WAR
THE KNIFE'S EDGE

NICK S. THOMAS

Copyright © 2023 Nick S. Thomas

All rights reserved.

ISBN: 979-8327196834

PROLOGUE

The two great Spanish fortresses of Ciudad Rodrigo and Badajoz have now fallen to Wellington's Anglo Portuguese army. They called the pair the keys to Spain, as they protected the two main roads and lines of communication from Portugal across the mostly mountainous border into Spain, which was almost entirely under the control of France.

With both keys unlocked, the door to Spain is wide open for the Anglo Portuguese army to march on to Madrid, the target of the Talavera campaign that alluded the allied army three years previously. Morale is high after two great successes, even in the face of such horrific casualties at the two bloody breaches. If the two French armies of Marmont and Soult had combined they could have been an unstoppable force, but trickery and deception on the part of Wellington's agents and the Spanish guerrillas ensured that had never happened. Soult had scurried off back to Cadiz, a siege which has dragged on for years and shows no sign of ending.

However, there is still one great obstacle on the road ahead. Marshal Marmont's army remains formidable and strong, and soon enough the time will come where Wellington's army would have to meet the almost thirty thousand strong army in open battle. The armies of Marmont and Wellington now seek one another out, but who is the hunter and who is the hunted? A victory for either side could be the defining moment of the year, and it may change the direction of the whole war.

CHAPTER 1

"Come on, Sir!" Paget cried.

They galloped along a beautiful valley without a care in the world. The capture of Badajoz had given breathing room for the entire army, and they were making the most of it. Portugal was safe, and finally momentum was in the hands of the Anglo Portuguese army. It felt like they had entered a new age. Craven smiled as he watched the Lieutenant race on with such joy and passion in his face. Craven spurred his horse on further. Life could not seem better as they had survived the assault of Badajoz; he had been reinstated with the rank of Major and absolved of the crimes he was accused. It seemed as though the sky was the limit. The sun was shining on a beautiful spring day, and there was not an enemy in sight.

"I'll race you to the top!" Paget pointed to a ridge line at the end of the valley ahead.

Craven was happy to indulge him, but he also knew the

race was a forgone conclusion. For Augustus was a fine horse indeed, and Paget weighed a fraction of Craven, but it didn't matter. Craven liked to win, but he had come to find great joy in seeing his closest friends come out on top. He shook his head as he thought back to when he and Paget first met and how much they had detested one another.

"Come on, Sir, you can do better!"

Craven gave it everything, but it was not nearly enough to catch Paget who vanished over the peak. Craven stormed on after him.

"You run away quicker and faster than a Spaniard!" Craven roared as he raced on over the same crest but brought his horse to an abrupt halt. He found Paget and Augustus had halted upon making it over the top.

"Christ, as you trying to kill me!" he cried out as his horse reared up uncontrollably before its hooves slammed back down to the ground. Craven looked to Paget as if to demand an explanation, but he said nothing and looked frozen to stone, except his eyes, which drew Craven's attention away. He followed the gaze to find Wellington himself looking out across the plains in the distance. He was alone in a melancholic state, his staff waiting thirty paces back, surely on his orders. The two riders had interrupted a most tranquil scene.

"My apologies, Sir," Paget finally blurted out.

Craven said nothing, but Wellington looked back with a smile.

"Come here," he insisted.

They both dismounted and led their horses on foot to the precarious ledge where Wellington had been deep in peaceful contemplation just moments before. Craven still walked with a limp from the bayonet he had received at the taking of Badajoz. He was lucky the blade had not pierced anything vital, for such a wound could kill. It did not go unnoticed by Wellington, though he said nothing. Neither Craven nor Paget spoke as they waited for their commander to address them. But he left them hanging with an uncomfortable silence, as if contemplating what their punishment should be. Finally, Wellington broke the silence to end their suffering.

"Do you know why I came here?"

Paget looked confused as if expecting a very different response, and most certainly not a question.

"To decide which way to go on?" Craven answered.

Wellington nodded in agreement.

"Not so literally, Major, but in essence you would be quite correct in your assumption. I came here to be alone with my thoughts, to look for a sign, for inspiration, and the world gives me you two. I would say I am surprised, and yet I am not. For you, Craven, manage to stumble your way into a great many things whether you should have or not."

"Yes, Sir," admitted Craven.

Wellington sighed before taking a deep breath in contemplation of the tough choice ahead of him.

"You have to meet the enemy in battle, and you must decide which one?"

Paget looked stunned that Craven would have such a grasp of the situation and the knowledge with which to make such a response to the General. Wellington looked almost as shocked also, but also pleased, as he went on.

"Two paths lie ahead. We may go South and strike at Soult who has scurried back to continue his investment of Cadiz, or

North after Marmont who gathers his strength to endanger Ciudad Rodrigo once more. Strike at Soult and we may free Cadiz and end French control in the South of Spain, or to Marmont and we have a chance at the main army in the country. What say you?"

Paget looked deeply uncomfortable, not wanting to have such pressure weighing on his shoulders, but Craven did not hesitate with his opinion.

"Cadiz has held for years, and it will continue to hold. Marmont is the target, but you already knew that, did you not, Sir?"

Wellington smiled.

"Why would you say so?" he asked curiously.

"Strike at Soult in the South and you must then march North to also engage Marmont, but if we can defeat Marmont first, then Soult will have no choice but to give up his efforts at Cadiz for fear of having his lines of communication to France entirely cut off. For with the Royal Navy in control of the sea, this has always been a war of the roads in Spain."

Wellington looked as stunned as Paget had been when they first stumbled upon the General.

"You have a keen eye and an equally keen mind, Craven. One which could be of great value to me, that is if you could pick fewer fights with the officers of this army. But I am curious, how did you know and see what so many around me could not?"

"Yes, Sir, how did you come up with this?" Paget pressed.

"There might be a great many things in the management of an army that I would not understand, but the choice before you, Sir, is no different to me with sword in hand facing two French soldiers before me. I do not blindly barrel into them nor choose my target merely by chance. I must ask which one is stronger, which one poses more of a danger, and what effect the defeat of one might have on the other, along with a great many other factors. The choices before you are no different, Sir."

"Do you reduce everything down to a duel?" Wellington smiled.

"Mostly, for a great many decisions are like a duel, just as the two paths before you now do battle with one another to determine the outcome, as two men do battle with swords."

Wellington looked most amused.

"So, Marmont it is, Sir?" Craven added.

Wellington barely moved his head up and down but a fraction and said nothing, but it was all the confirmation they needed to know the answer.

"I knew which was the best path, but so much depends on what we do here, and I could not risk making the wrong decision rashly."

"Sir, Major Craven says you make no mistakes in a fight, or you never let anyone see that you did. You commit to a course and keep moving forward, ensuring your opponent is as confident of your victory as you are, or more over, never let them think you made a misstep. Everything you do was as intended, whether it was or was not," declared Paget.

"Gentlemen, as I tell many an officer of this army, there is no mistake, there has been no mistake; and there shall be no mistake. Some take it to mean that a man must be perfect in all things, but I am glad to see that you men see the other side. When other generals make mistakes, their armies are beaten. When I get into a hole, my men pull me out of it," he smiled.

"Yes, Sir," Paget replied proudly.

"Do you know Napoleon has set off to the East from Paris with a great army?"

"I had heard the rumours, Sir," admitted Craven.

"Then he means to conquer, and in doing so he weakens himself here in Spain. He has appointed his brother, King Joseph, to be commander in chief across all of Spain, in an attempt to quell the bickering and muddle amongst the French commanders."

"Has it worked, Sir?" Paget asked.

Wellington smirked. "Messages we have intercepted suggest the same old problems remain."

"Then we march North to face Marmont?"

"Indeed. You are in fact right, Craven. I had made my decision, but it is a welcome sound to hear others are of the same mind. To hear it from capable officers bolsters one's faith in oneself."

"Then this is it, Sir? We finally march to fight the principal French army in Spain to finish them once and for all?" Paget asked excitedly.

"That is indeed my intention, and we will do everything in our power to make it a reality."

"Then we will finally march into Madrid?"

"Yes, but not as conquerors, but to a triumphant welcome as liberators," replied Wellington.

Paget looked out into the distance with a smile as he dreamed of such a day.

"Let us not celebrate before the work is done, gentlemen."

"What can we do, Sir?" Craven asked.

"For now, we enjoy something we have not done since the start, greater numbers than the enemy. I have more than forty thousand soldiers at the ready and even the promise of Spanish help for what it's worth. Marmont is weak, and so is Soult. But together they could be strong, and even alone both Marshals will be able to call upon more troops once they hear of our movements towards them."

"Then they must never know of the movements of this army, not until it is too late."

"Yes. Soon the army will march, but for its success we must have the enemy in complete disillusionment, not knowing where we will strike and when."

"Creating chaos is what I do best," smiled Craven.

"Indeed. I am sending General Hill to the bridge at Almaraz. It cannot be overstated how important this place it to both our troops and to the enemy. The French have built a pontoon bridge at Almaraz, and it is well fortified on both banks of the Tagus."

"Almaraz, Sir?" Craven was unfamiliar with the place and its importance.

"Almaraz is the only place Marshal Soult could hope to cross the Tagus if he was to march north to support Marmont. It lies halfway between Badajoz and Ciudad Rodrigo, on the Spanish side. Destroy the bridge at Almaraz and we keep the French armies from gathering their strength together."

"Whilst we will maintain the threat of attacking both North and South, for we can move through Portugal when they cannot, Sir?" replied Paget.

"Precisely. We will cut them off and then we will cause chaos. Craven, I want you to assist at Almaraz. Whatever happens there the bridge must fall, and when it does, I want you to run free and wild. All across the Spain I have asked that regular and guerrilla forces alike step up their efforts against the French. We must keep them in the dark and stop them from gathering their strength. Do what you do best, Major, but only for a few short weeks, three or four at most, for then you must ride North. For when we meet Marmont in open battle, I would have you there on that field of battle."

"I am not sure I can make all the difference in an affair fought by near fifty thousand of our soldiers, Sir."

"No, Major, but you carry good luck with you. I have never relied on luck, but I shall take all the advantages I can into this endeavour, and I will have you there, do you hear me?"

"Yes, Sir."

"Thank you, gentlemen, and good luck," replied Wellington. He then marched away at a formidable pace, confident in his assessments and decisions.

"Sir, did we just decide that?" began Paget, a little pale-faced that they might have influenced the entire course of the war.

"We did nothing of the sort. There is not an opinion in the land which would change that man's heart. No, he had long decided on a course of action before our arrival."

Paget breathed a sigh of relief, for he did not ever want to much pressure resting on his shoulders.

"Almaraz it is, then," mused Craven as he looked out into the distance just as Wellington had when they first came upon the General.

"I hear the French have very heavily fortified the place, Sir. For we partially destroyed the bridge at the start of our campaign in 1809, and the Spanish had done a similar job not long before. The enemy must surely know the great importance of the place just as we do."

"Yes, but they are also blind to all that we do, and we must continue to keep them that way."

"Blind, Sir?"

"Just as Thorny has always said, this is a war of information. Wellington knows where everything is, of our troops, of our allies, and of the enemy forces. But the French armies have a near complete block in communication, not knowing what we will do and where. It is a weapon more valuable to Wellington than ten thousand soldiers or more. That is how we can make a difference. How a force as small as ours can continue to achieve far more than our number might suggest, by denying the enemy a chance to gather their great strength where it is needed."

Craven took out a folded map from inside his jacket as Paget leaned in close to a good look himself.

"Almaraz." Craven pointed to it on the map. It was as far East into Spain as Salamanca was, just further South. It was the only sizeable crossing for a French army for hundreds of miles.

"A big step on towards Madrid, we will be fighting through the Extremadura once more," declared Paget.

Craven's eyebrow elevated a little at the mention of the region.

"What is it, Sir?"

"Just like Wellington said, we are not marching into enemy lands, but liberating our allies. We have friends in Spain, and we must not forget it."

"You have friends all around it would seem, Sir, for what a day we live in."

"How so? What is your meaning?"

"Your life was saved by Timmerman of all people. Timmerman! The same Timmerman who did not loot and rape at Badajoz as I would have bet my fortune on him doing, and how others wearing this uniform did, those wretches. This war has made a good man of him. You have made a good man of him, and we now count that man amongst our friends, and thank God. For I most certainly did not much enjoy having him as our enemy."

"It has changed us all."

"Truly, Sir?" Paget was fishing for more revelations.

Craven smiled and obliged as he no longer had anything to hide from the young Lieutenant who had come to be one of his closest friends.

"I hated you when we first met. I hated your blind optimism and loyalty to England. I hated how good you were at heart. I didn't believe it could be true and somehow was merely an act. It took me a long time to realize that your heart is truer than any other. Never change, Berkeley, for you are the best of us."

Paget was stunned and close to tears and could find no words for a few seconds.

"I cannot truly explain what it means to hear you say it, Sir, but I can say that none of this would have been possible without your leadership. I know you have always seen yourself as a swordsman. A lonely fighter trying to make his own way, and no one can ever doubt your prowess with a sword, but that is not what has got you this far nor earned you the rank you hold today. You are a leader, Sir, and we all see it, even Lord Wellington."

The sound of Wellington and his staff's horses riding away

into the distance was suddenly replaced by another set approaching at speed. They turned back and saw General Le Marchant approaching with a dozen of his cavalrymen.

"I thought it was you!" The General excitedly came to a halt before them.

"The peace following Badajoz gave us quite the opportunity for a peaceful ride through this beautiful country, but the day has ended quite differently than one might expect," smiled Craven.

"Wellington's given you some work to do, has he?" Le Marchant laughed.

"And then some," admitted Craven.

Le Marchant looked down to Craven's side to see he was still wearing the broadly curved light cavalry officer's sabre made by Gill that he had gifted him. Its bare iron scabbard gleamed in the sunlight.

"I see I have won you over at last," smiled Gaspard.

"It is the right tool for the job at hand," admitted Craven.

"Quite, and don't let anyone ever tell you otherwise. I know what I am doing in the saddle, just as you could defeat any one of my men on foot. I showed you how it is done from the saddle and gave you a sword with which you can defeat any man from it. One day I would very much appreciate you doing the same for me from down there on the ground."

"The heavy cavalry, Sir, they wear a sword much like your Andrea Ferrara when dismounted or in dress," declared Paget.

"Your man is correct, and if you would do me such an honour, I would be most grateful."

"I can teach you, Sir, anytime that we have some free moments, but finding a sword as capable as my own and worthy of a gift, I cannot say, for it is no easy task."

"You mean it will come at a great cost?" Le Marchant asked.

"Well...yes that, too."

Le Marchant took out a coin purse from his saddle and tossed it at Craven. He caught the weighty bag.

"Find me a sword the great swordsman Major Craven would consider worthy, and when you do, we shall endeavour to continue our practice."

Craven was stunned as he opened up the purse to find such a great sum of money. It was more than he could ever hope to have in his hands.

"You trust me with this?"

"No, not entirely, but I like to think I have the measure of a man once I have crossed swords with him. Find me a sword, Craven, one which I will wear upon our triumphant march into Paris!"

"Yes, Sir."

"Good luck, Craven."

"And to you, Sir."

Once again Craven and Paget were left alone on the vantage point where Wellington had come to contemplate all their futures.

"Where will you find such a fine sword, Sir?"

Craven shrugged. "Great swords were once made in Toledo, but I do not know what we will find there in these times."

"Then we must look to the enemy, Sir, for they bring a great deal of weapons into Spain."

"You would have me take a sword from the enemy, and

not purchase it for the General?" Craven asked in amazement as he looked at the heavy purse of money.

"The General requested that you find him a magnificent sword, but he did not say how nor make any mention of making a purchase."

Craven smiled, for he never thought he would hear Paget be so sneaky.

"And if I can find a sword without spending any of this?"

"Then it would be a great payment for services rendered, Sir."

Craven was stunned that the wealthy young man was finally starting to appreciate how everyone else lived. Craven tucked the purse carefully away into his jacket. He mounted his horse once more and took a final glance out across the beautiful view that Wellington had come to observe.

"Extremadura it is, then. We have waited for this moment ever since we withdrew after Talavera. Years have passed. Hard years. But here we are, the gates of Spain are open to us, and now we take our turn."

"We must carry the news back to the Salfords. I'll race you!"

Paget leapt onto his beloved horse and wheeled about, launching into a rapid pace. Craven smiled for he knew he could not keep up, but he enjoyed the challenge, nonetheless. He took one last glance to the East across the vast landscape before them.

"It is our turn indeed," he repeated to himself before wheeling his horse about and soaring on after Paget.

CRAVEN'S WAR – THE KNIFE'S EDGE

CHAPTER 2

"Come on, then!" a voice roared as Craven and Paget rode back into camp. They could see Matthys and Amyn stripping off to their shirts ready to fight.

"Not this again," complained Craven.

He thought they had settled their conflict. Craven increased the pace of his horse as he braced himself to break up another fight, but as they drew closer, he noticed the two swordsmen take up singlesticks to conduct a friendly contest. He breathed a sigh of relief and finally relaxed once more as they dismounted and tied up their mounts. He had to leave Paget behind, for the young officer would not leave his beloved horse without a few soothing words.

Craven watched as Amyn and Matthys went at it. They fought with speed and precision, but not power. They were not trying to do one another harm, for it was a contest of speed with respect for one another. He watched with glee as the fight went on. The two looked closely matched and increasingly like a mirror of the other as each man learnt the other's ways and tried to use it against them. They went on and on for several minutes without a single blow landing until finally, a natural pause came as they took a breather.

"Shall we call it a draw?" Amyn asked.

"Yes," gasped Matthys who was running out of steam.

The two men embraced with a firm handshake. It was a welcome sight.

"Well fought!"

Both fighters had been so intently focused on their contest that they had not noticed his return.

"What news?" Matthys asked as he wiped sweat from his face.

"What makes you think I bring news?"

"Because you left for a casual ride, and you have returned with much on your mind."

Craven tried to shrug it off.

"Come on, James, you cannot hide these things from me," insisted Matthys.

"Fair enough," he admitted.

"Well, what is it, then?"

Craven looked around cautiously to ensure nobody was listening in.

"Wellington intends to march North and engage Marmont."

"Yes," replied Matthys as if he already knew.

"How did you know that?"

"Because it is the best course of action," replied Matthys confidently.

"And yet Soult is still a threat." Craven took out his battered little map, "But we aren't marching North, not yet." He then pointed to the map, "Our task is to assist General Hill here, at the bridge of Almaraz."

Matthys nodded along in agreement.

"Clever," he admitted.

"You think so?" Craven asked as if setting him a trap.

"Yes, Almaraz is a pontoon bridge, set up by the French to replace the one we destroyed before it. With the capture of Badajoz, we also took Soult's pontoon train, and so if we destroy the bridge at Almaraz he cannot replace it. All supplies and troop movements will be forced to move far to the East and only strain the enemy further whilst prohibiting Soult from coming to the aid of Marmont, and vice versa."

Craven nodded along as if he knew all that Matthys had said, but the truth was Matthys was better informed than he was.

"Wellington wants us to assist with Almaraz and then in divisionary attacks and attacks on French communication lines after it. But he also wants us back with the army within a few weeks, before the great battle which is long overdue."

"Then we should take only those who are mounted and send the rest of the Salford Rifles on with Wellington."

Craven nodded in appreciation of Matthys' tactical mind.

"Good, I should want to remain fast and flexible after we depart from General Hill's force."

"I see you are confident in overcoming Almaraz?"

"Should I not be?"

"Oh, no, you very much should be. For we certainly need success, but it will be no easy feat. The bridge at Almaraz is not any pontoon bridge, but a vital road that the French are very much aware of."

"And?"

"It is heavily defended and fortified on both sides of the river. Forts, a stone tower, redoubt. A fortified bridgehead and additional defences all around. Only a few miles to the South the French hold a castle which will assist in the defence of the bridge. This could be a siege in its own right."

"But the enemy believe we want the bridge," smiled Craven as he went on, "Two boats form the centre of the bridge and are removed for security often at night or if danger is imminent. The enemy believe we want to take that bridge."

"And we do not?"

"No, we will burn it to the ground. We do not need it, but to the enemy it is worth its weight in gold."

"Soult will know its value, and that is why the enemy have so heavily fortified the place. They could have one or maybe even two thousand men protecting the bridge at Almaraz, and guns, too."

"I don't think Hill nor Wellington have a prolonged affair in mind. We will move quickly and take the enemy by surprise before they even know we are coming for them."

"It will take many thousands of men to have any chance of success here. You think a body of soldiers that large can move in secrecy?"

"You have seen how cut off the enemy are. The French have to move in great numbers if they are to move anywhere. Their lines of communication are barely existent now."

Matthys shrugged.

"It is not for me to say either way, anyway. If these are our orders, then I will see them done. When do we depart?"

"At first light."

"Then let us enjoy one more night in peace before we depart."

Craven looked backed to their encampment to see everyone going about their lives as best they could. The Salford Rifles seemed to be in good spirits, and that was understandable. Success at Badajoz was a great relief to them all, and they had suffered few casualties, unlike many of the infantry regiments that had assaulted the breaches directly.

"Do you think they know? That we are setting off once more?"

"Of course. There is not a soldier in this army who expected us to stop once the spring came, so long as we could continue to succeed at least."

"I'd like to say it is going to be easy, but it won't be. Wellington says he finally has an army which outnumbers any one of the French army's here in Spain, but it is still only one army against all that they have."

"When you dominated as a stage gladiator, do you think you could defeat all of the fighters in England at the same time?"

"Of course not."

"No, you knocked them down one after the other, and that is what Wellington is doing, too."

"Yes, but I never fought with so much at stake," sighed Craven.

"Not as a gladiator, no, but as a Captain and as a Major you most certainly have."

Craven nodded with appreciation.

"Enough of this, for it is tomorrow's task. Let us make the most of the time we have left before then."

"Certainly, for we have wine, so much wine."

"What? How?"

"You will have to ask Captain Ferreira." He then pointed to a party of the Portuguese riflemen making merry as others flocked to them to get their fill.

Craven licked his lips as he approached.

"Here, Major!" Charlie called out, handing him a cup of wine as she was carrying two.

He looked impressed as he pushed on towards Ferreira.

"Where did you find it?"

"Gifts from the Lady Sarmento for the entire regiment," he replied gleefully.

"She sent it to you?" Craven asked accusingly, knowing the Lady would almost certainly have addressed such a gift to himself.

"Well…no, to you, but you were nowhere to be found, and I thought I should lead by your example and not wait idly by."

Craven laughed as nothing could be truer and more accurate. But Ferreira's smile quickly vanished as he realised there was something major weighing on Craven's mind.

"It's time, isn't it? Time for us to advance once more?" he asked quietly.

Craven nodded in agreement.

"Well, we all knew the time would come. Which army to we march for?"

"Neither?"

"Oh?" Craven stepped away from the others so that they might speak more privately.

"Those on foot will march North in the hope of finding

Marmont, but I will lead a mounted party in support of General Hill."

"To where?"

"The bridge at Almaraz."

Ferreira's eyebrows elevated as he clearly knew the danger posed by the fortified position as well as Matthys did.

"Yes, yes, I have heard it all already," pre-empted Craven.

"I had just hoped we were done with the assaulting of walls. We excel out there, amongst the trees and villages and even the open plains, but in a gruelling siege and assault our skills and our talents are wasted, and perhaps our lives, too."

"Almaraz can be no prolonged siege. It is no siege at all, but a rapid assault. This is not a city we must take, nor some resources we must capture. We are a raiding party with only one goal, and that is destruction."

"Then you are the perfect man for the job," smiled Ferreira.

Craven laughed once more as they clashed cups and had their fill.

"We must not forget the sword for the General Le Marchant, Sir." Paget had joined them.

"Which sword is this?" Ferreira asked.

"The General requested Major Craven purchase him a sword fit for combat on foot."

"Acquire, however we go about it is our business," insisted Craven.

"The General gave a weighty purse for the endeavour."

"Its loss will mean nothing to a man like that," declared Ferreira.

"How so?" Paget enquired.

"Le Marchant was born into the wealthiest family in Guernsey. He even has the ear of the King, you know. A purse of money is a mere trinket to a man like that."

Craven was taken aback how he might know so much about an English officer.

"And how would you come to know all of that?"

"How could you not?"

Craven shrugged as he did have some inclination, but not to the certainty with which Ferreira did.

"I imagine an officer would do well to have friends in the cavalry, for soon enough this war will be fought in open ground where they will be invaluable," added Paget.

"No doubt, if we can ever meet the enemy in open battle that man will be a great asset to us all. He is just the sort of cavalry commander this army needs to ride on to Madrid and beyond."

"And to Paris, Sir?" Paget asked excitedly.

"Let's not get ahead of ourselves, but yes, it is always the dream, isn't it?"

"The French marched all the way to Lisbon. I would return the favour," smirked Ferreira.

None of the others came to search for news from Craven as they made merry of the evening without a care in the world.

"Should we inform them of our departure, Sir?" Paget asked.

"No, let them have this night."

"There will be some sore heads in the morning," replied Matthys.

"And you think they would show any more restraint if they knew we marched tomorrow?"

"Not a chance."

"Momentum is finally in our favour, isn't it?" Craven sighed in relief.

"For the moment, but whether we can make best advantage of it remains to be seen. Spain is a big country and the French still have several armies here. We have to strike a decisive blow and quickly, or Rodrigo and Badajoz will have been for nothing."

Craven sighed once more, this time with exhaustion, but Matthys went on.

"Wellington knows this. In fact, I think most of the army knows this by now. Everything we have done in this new year was to open the gates for us to do what we must do now."

"Badajoz was our last chance. That is what they said. That is what I said, too."

"Yes, our last chance to break out into Spain and see that victory might be a possibility."

"And is it?"

"More so than ever. Napoleon weakens his forces here in Spain to support whatever ridiculous campaign he is about to embark on to the North. Wellington has a great army under his command, and for the first time since it all began, the numbers are in our favour."

"Then there is hope?"

"Come on, Craven, you know there is, but more than anything it is down to what is in here." He pointed to his heart, "So much of what a man can do comes down to what he believes he can do. You taught me that."

"I am not sure I can claim credit."

"Yes, yes you can. For all of your faults, that is one of your greatest strengths. You believe in yourself, you believe in others, and you are not afraid to let them know it. It means the world to them all. These soldiers of the Salfords, they are not here because of this war. They are here because of you. Because you inspire them and drive them to be far better than they ever dreamed possible."

"I thought that was your job?" Craven smiled at him.

"And so did I, but it was you all along. I am merely here to guide you so that you stay on the path that you were destined to walk."

"And you think this is destiny?"

"Perhaps, but that does not mean it can happen without work. You have fought for every inch of the life you now lead, and you should be proud of yourself."

"I always was," smirked Craven.

"As a fighter that is true, but now you have something far greater to be proud of. Who you are as a man."

Craven chuckled a little but soon fell into a deep reflection as he realised Matthys' words were heartfelt and true.

He awoke the next day feeling remarkably fresh. He had not gorged himself on the wine as he always had, although he had thought about Matthys' words before going to bed. He looked out across the camp. Few had arisen, though Charlie and Paget approached.

"This is it, then?" she asked.

"You shared army movements?" Craven asked Paget accusingly.

"I would never risk such information, Sir, but neither would I hide it from those I trust most," he snapped back in his own defence.

Craven looked unimpressed.

"Come on, Craven, we all know," added Charlie.

"Then you know where we are heading?"

"Of course, a dangerous target, but we will see it done."

"Yes, we will."

"I don't much like dividing our numbers. These are not just soldiers under my command, but my friends, but it must be done."

"We will be reunited soon enough," declared Charlie.

"Up! Get up!" Matthys shouted as he stomped through the camp. They watched as the troops begrudgingly arose.

"Berkeley tells me you are in search of a sword for General Le Marchant?"

Craven looked judgingly at Paget for having spilled all of his secrets to Charlie.

"Don't pay for it, please, for we will find you a sword worthy of the General."

Paget now looked as put out as Craven. He wasn't at all comfortable with the sword not being purchased with the monies provided.

"Oh, I don't mean to," smiled Craven, much to the discomfort of Paget.

The mounted element of the Salfords were soon preparing to depart whilst the others remained in camp with the army. They awaited their orders as Craven approached Ferreira who was busy preparing his saddle.

"Ready for this?" asked his Portuguese friend.

But the look on Craven's face made him realise something was amiss.

"You don't want me to come, do you?"

Craven nodded in agreement, causing Ferreira to sigh in frustration.

"I would want you there by my side, believe me, but the men need you. I cannot leave Gamboa in command whilst they remain with the army. They need you, and Quental, too, to support you."

"You would make a raid without two of the best riflemen at your disposal?"

"If rifles are needed, then we are already in trouble."

"You are always in trouble."

Craven laughed, for it was true. Ferreira didn't like it, but he respected the decision, and as he looked out to the rest of the regiment, he knew it to be true.

"I'll stay," he declared.

"Thank you, I was hoping to not have to fight you on this one."

"You go on a dangerous mission without any rewards. I think I'll stay with the army," he smiled.

But Craven knew he was merely making light of the situation, as in truth he cared greatly.

"No speeches. As far as the army is concerned, the mounted element of the Salfords is leaving on scouting duties. For the enemy have their spies the same as we do."

"Of course."

A little over thirty soldiers gathered their equipment and mounted their horses to depart. They travelled light with only a few days provisions and powder, just as a scouting party might need, but in truth it was all they hoped they would need at Almaraz. They could not afford a protracted affair. They departed without any ceremony, but word had already spread amongst the Salford Rifles, and every one of them knew what lay in their future. They rode on at a robust pace, and by the end of the second day Hill's force was in sight setting up camp without tents in a most primitive fashion. Craven led the advance toward the sentries and identified himself, yet he was not permitted to pass.

"Let them through!"

It was Thornhill who appeared out from the shadows of a few trees nearby.

"Thorny? Of course, this operation had your scent all over it," declared Craven.

"And that is why I asked for you, Major," he smiled.

"It was Wellington who requested our participation in this operation."

"Of course," Thorny smirked.

"That will do." Craven pointed to a quiet spot for them to make camp far from the rest of the army. He dismounted and passed the reins of his horse to Joze before following Major Thornhill on. They passed a line of nine artillery pieces, which were kept well-guarded. He was led to a circle of officers sitting beside a fire with General Hill outlining their plan. The town of Almaraz was mapped out with rocks on the ground, and the river by several branches.

"I present Major Craven," declared Thorny.

"Yes, I am aware of who he is."

"Lord Wellington sent me to support you, Sir."

"I believe we have fought over the same ground you and I, at Bussaco I should think?"

"Yes, Sir."

"I can't say I requested you, Major, but the extra hands are welcome, and it is also a welcome chance to be going toward the enemy rather than fleeing from them, wouldn't you say?"

"I would, Sir."

"How many men do you bring?"

"A little over thirty, Sir."

Several of the officers laughed, but not Hill, which soon brought them to silence.

"I do not need the most men for what we must do, but I do need the best. Wellington assures me that you are made of such stuff, is that true?"

"Major Craven's results speak for themselves," snapped Thorny in defence of Wellington.

"I think a man of the Major's reputation can speak for himself, can he not?" Hill replied firmly.

"Yes," replied Thorny begrudgingly.

"Well, Major?"

"I came here to fight, and I do it well, better than most."

"Good, for we are up against it. We will have the element of surprise up to a point, but six thousand men cannot remain a secret forever, and should the enemy manage to alert the rest of their armies in Spain to our presence, they might rain down hell upon us."

"You don't mean to use those guns, do you?" Craven thought of the artillery pieces they had passed.

Hill smiled as he drew out his sword and pointed to each piece of the primitive map on the ground.

"The pontoon bridge at Almaraz is a robust one of about two hundred yards long and with two centre boats, which are removed at night for security of the crossing of the Tagus, a most valuable one to the enemy. On the North bank is Fort

Ragusa, and on the South bank an even greater defence, Fort Napoleon. Six miles to the South the enemy have built further defences housing gun emplacements connected to a well defended castle. Miravete it is called. It was merely a tower, but the enemy have enhanced the defences of every part. Every emplacement that the enemy have built is significant and strong with ditches, palisades, and all manner of works. It is no Badajoz, but it is a great obstacle in its own right. The enemy have effectively made that bridge a fortress."

"Which tells us how important it is to them," added Craven.

"Quite right, a mighty fortress, and yet what the French do not have for all of their walls and guns, they do not have enough soldiers. They are spread thin. A thousand soldiers guard that bridge, perhaps fifteen hundred. We do not have their defences, nor do we have their guns, nor is time on our side. But for once, we have superiority in numbers. We will roll over them in a great wave, attacking from all sides so the enemy may not concentrate their numbers in any one point. Almaraz is prepared to stand against investment. They believe time is on their side."

"A direct assault? Just like Wellington did upon arrival at Ciudad Rodrigo, Sir?" Craven asked.

"Perhaps. I know these villages, hills, and mountains well, but the fortifications that the enemy have constructed I do not know. All information regarding these works has been provided by the local people here in Spain. As useful information as it is, it is not nearly detailed nor accurate enough to plan a siege nor an assault. We will advance on Almaraz and let this situation unfold as is best as we encounter it. Surprise, gentlemen, it is the word of the day, and let us keep it until the very last moment.

You all know what you have to do."

"I do not."

"Where would you wish to go, Major Craven?"

Craven thought about it for a few moments before smiling.

"Fort Napoleon?" General Hill asked.

Craven nodded in agreement.

"Then you are with me. Good luck, gentlemen. Get what rest you can before we part ways. For when next we meet it will be as we descend upon the enemy as one. Good luck."

CHAPTER 3

Craven gasped as he stopped to catch his breath and wipe the sweat from his brow. He looked around with despair as it was dark, and he would very much like to rest his eyes, even on the rough ground. But instead, they were making their advance through the mountains towards the valley of Almaraz. All around he could hear the groans of soldiers battling with the rugged paths, hacking their way through foliage and struggling over jagged and uneven terrain, which was hard to see in the moonlight, having had to leave their forces behind as they traversed the difficult terrain on their own feet. Finally, daybreak came. They were not even halfway down the final mountain side and the orders were passed to withdraw. Craven shook his head in disbelief but for the first time he got a glance at their target. The terrain was inhospitable all around with only a single road approaching the bridge from the South, the same road which was protected by Miravete and a series of other defensive works.

The only other routes into the valley were little more than goat paths. As for the bridge itself, it was as Hill had feared, if not worse. Strong ditches and palisades had been built with parapets and even towers. A sizeable number of French troops patrolled them, with many more surely waiting to be called up at short notice.

They withdrew to a place of sanctuary far from the enemy's gaze. As Craven approached the tired troops who had sat or laid down to rest, he could see Hill and many other officers gathered about. He had stretched a map out over the floor and drawn over it in pencil to mark out the enemy positions he had witnessed with his own eyes, or had such information passed to him by those officers under his command.

"Not the best of starts, Major," said Hill as Craven approached, seemingly looking to him for advice.

"And the other columns?"

Hill used a stick to point out the routes the three different columns had taken.

"General Chowne with his column ascended the ridge and advanced on Miravete, but they found it to be even more strongly defended than we could have expected, and with the difficulty of the terrain no guns could be brought up. The centre column advanced only to find the defences built along the road are equally as strong, and well, we did not fare any better on these damn mountains. All hope of a surprise is over, and we have not yet found a way to bring our guns up. We might lower the guns down the bank into the valley, but it will be a long and difficult operation that could put us in a perilous position."

"We cannot go through that valley without assaulting every defence and overcoming it first," declared Craven.

"The enemy will know that, too," insisted Paget as he interrupted.

"We cannot manage that, not in the time we have, and it will come at a great cost, too," Craven added.

"I do not mean to," replied Hill confidently.

"Sir?" Craven asked.

"A protracted affair will only draw reinforcements from the enemy here, at Talavera, barely fifty miles to the East."

Paget's eyes rolled back in amazement. He had no idea they had come so close to that hallow ground they had fought so hard for years before. Hill went on.

"The enemy is strong in all places, but in doing so they spread their forces thinly, and all that matters is that bridge and the forts at either end of it. The goat path through Ramangorda here to the East is passable. I know it is tough, but with an early start at dawn and sheer determination, I am confident a column of infantry could make a dashing assault with only ladders against Fort Napoleon."

"It could work, but we will want enemy eyes elsewhere until the very last moment," replied Craven.

"Chowne will commence a false attack on Miravete, firing with every gun and ensuring all of his strength is seen by the enemy."

"But they cannot make any headway against Miravete, not even with those twenty-four-pounders," declared Paget.

"No, but they do not have to. All our efforts will be made at Fort Napoleon. I wondered what purpose you might have here, Craven, but now I am certain that I know it. This will not be a prolonged affair. It must not be. This fight will be won by cold steel. A brave dash to the walls of the fort, and a struggle with sword and bayonet to secure the walls and push on. Speed is of the essence. When this thing gets underway it must not stop. There must be no hesitation, no exchanges of volleys, nor any other obstacle."

"There will be a great many of those at the fort, for the enemy have many layers of defensive works."

"Wellington tells me you are at your very best when you must overcome the unexpected. This is what we need now more than ever. Will you be there with us? Will you take cold steel to the enemy?"

Craven looked anxious for a moment, being the first to assault a fortification was a horrifying prospect after all they had witnessed at Rodrigo and Badajoz. Paget could see it in his eyes, as he was thinking the same.

"This will not be another Badajoz. The enemy do not have the slightest idea we are coming," he insisted.

Craven appreciated the sentiment.

"Then we all know what must be done. Everything hinges on Fort Napoleon. It is all that matters. For everything else is merely a sound and a light show for the enemy," declared Hill.

"Yes, Sir," replied Craven.

He went back to the small force he commanded, many of which were his closest friends. Some were already asleep from exhaustion and others were not far behind. Yet Matthys, despite being the oldest amongst them, was proudly on his feet awaiting news or orders.

"Get some rest. Tonight we make a descent once more, but this time we know where we are going, and we will not be turning back."

They all knew what that would mean. An advance without

guns in place and a prior bombardment meant only one thing, and that was an impending assault. Birback was already snoring whilst Charlie sighed at the prospect.

"You do not approve?"

"Far from it, I'd rather get a chance at the French sooner than later," she replied.

"I agree. The waiting is the worst," agreed Paget.

Though Craven could see Charlie's reasons were very different from Paget's.

It was a tense wait throughout the day, and none could get as much rest as they would like and really needed. The anticipation and heat kept them wide awake, except for Birback, who snored through the rest of the day in complete tranquillity. Soon enough the time came for them to progress to their starting positions. The sun was very low in the sky, and night would soon provide all the concealment they needed to enact their plan. Even now Birback continued to snore, having slept through almost the entirety of the day.

"Somebody wake him up," complained Craven.

Charlie was happy to oblige and gave him a sharp kick. The Scotsman awoke but calmly as if not even noticing the blow.

"We finally moving?" he asked as he sat up.

Charlie shook her head in disbelief.

"We are, on your feet!" Paget roared.

Although he did not want to be too harsh on the man. They had learnt a begrudging respect for one another, despite the fact they could not be further apart in upbringing and personality. They were unified by one thing alone, fighting. They went on to the edge of the sierra which overlooked the town and the fortified bridge at Almaraz. It was much the same view they had encountered upon their first attempt at progressing towards the French positions, but this time they started earlier and with a path in mind, even if it was a treacherous one. It was 9pm and the last light of the day was fading away. The order was spread and on they went. It would be a long night, but progress was being made. At first light Craven stopped to get a good look at the fort which seemed almost in reach now.

"The boats have been moved, Sir," said Paget who also looked on with his own spyglass.

Craven nodded in agreement.

"The enemy must have spotted us, for they should be in place throughout the day."

"Do you think the enemy know our intentions, Sir?"

"To some extent, yes, but we must go on and hope that this advance has not been discovered."

The British guns echoed out in the distance as round and case shot against the castle of Miravete. Craven turned back to see French troops amassing at the walls of Fort Napoleon to watch with anticipation as their defences were assaulted.

"The enemy, Sir, they are amassing," said Paget.

But Craven smiled as he observed them.

"That does not concern you, Sir?"

"They do not gather for the defence, but to watch," he smiled.

Paget shrugged before realising what that meant.

"We are not discovered, Sir?" he asked with glee.

"Indeed."

On they went under the roar of the British guns, which drew all eyes to the South, as the infantry column made its way closer and closer to Fort Napoleon from the Southeast under the concealment of the rolling hills that lay before the walls. They formed up in readiness for what might come. There was no rush as they could not be seen by the Fort in the undulations of the land as the entire force formed up to advance as one.

In the light of day, Craven could now see what the force comprised of. Redcoats of the 50th Foot and 71st Highland Light Infantry, the 92nd Highlanders. Riflemen from the 60th and Portuguese Caçadores. There were blue-coated gunners of the Royal Artillery amongst the party, too, but without their guns, which could not be carried down the rugged terrain. Even the assault ladders had to be cut in half to be able to get around the winding path down the mountain side.

"What are they for?" Paget was looking to the gunners without their guns and only their short swords and muskets as if to act as infantry, a task they were not well suited to, and would be a waste.

Craven looked over to General Hill and the Brigade commander General Howard as they peered out towards the Fort from the ridge ahead. Craven smiled as he knew exactly what the gunners were for.

"They aren't here to man our guns, but those of the enemy."

Paget almost choked, as that seemed like wishful thinking.

"Wait here," insisted Craven.

Craven went to the front to see for himself and knelt down before creeping up the embankment beside the two most senior officers.

"Well, Craven, what do you say?" Hill asked.

Craven could barely believe his eyes as he got a good look for himself. They were just half a mile from the walls of Fort

Napoleon, and the enemy were still completely oblivious to them, focusing all their attention on the artillery bombardment of Miravete. They appeared most comfortable, firm in the knowledge that a few British guns could not overcome the position anytime soon.

"Ripe for the taking, Sir."

"Then let us not squander the opportunity."

Craven scurried back down the embankment and had only just reached his comrades when the general advance was given. Soldiers of the 50th and 71st led the advance forward over the last obstacle which concealed them. The redcoats were marching forward at a steady pace in the gleaming sunlight for all to see as though they went on to parade, with the green, brown, and blue coats of the Riflemen and Gunners in support. It was a grand spectacle as they moved aggressively forward. They could see the look of panic and bewilderment on the faces of many of the French troops who had gathered at the walls to watch the seemingly distant battle. For a moment they did not even move as if thinking they were seeing a mirage. For it seemed impossible that an Anglo Portuguese army had appeared before them.

"Onwards, boys!" Hill ordered.

Finally, they could hear the cries of Frenchmen as the seriousness of the situation dawned upon them. They hurried to prepare themselves, but the attacking force was just three hundred yards out from the walls. Musket fire echoed out from the walls as the first shots were levelled at the assaulting force, but it was not enough to deter them.

"Come on, boys!"

The pace increased as they rushed on the final distance. A

withering fire struck many soldiers down, but after Badajoz it didn't seem so bad at all. They reached the first ditch and leapt in eagerly, only to find their cut down ladders were too short to reach the parapets above. Yet not one man panicked at the prospect as they placed the ladders up to the first earthen ledge, scrambling up and hoisting more ladders up to make the final ascent in a two-stage affair. Musket fire rained down from the enemy above, but the assault had a great momentum behind it, and the soldiers would not be deterred. A brave Captain of the 50th was first over the top. He was then struck down by several French musket balls, but that enraged his fellow soldiers further as they climbed atop the ramparts.

All fear Craven harboured of what a siege and an assault could be faded away, for he knew almost all of that savagery could be avoided if they could get the job done quickly.

"Come on!"

He darted up one of the ladders and climbed the second one even more quickly. He leapt up onto the parapet to find only three other redcoats had made it and were engaging in a brutal close combat affair with bayonet and the butts of their muskets. He did not even have time to draw his pistol but took up the sword, which was fixed to his wrist by his sword knot. He grabbed hold of a Frenchmen's musket and drove him back into two others whilst running one of them through.

Birback was the next man over and to Craven's disbelief he was empty-handed, but that did not seem to bother him as there was a joyous excitement in his eyes. He was not even filled with rage, for he was having too much fun, as if he were some crazed pirate who had just boarded his latest prize. The great Scotsman grabbed hold of a French soldier and merely picked him up. He then tossed him over the parapet, where he would meet certain death at the hands of the assaulters even if he did survive the fall. One British soldier leapt over the rampart with a large axe in hand, the sort a pioneer might use and could be quite useful during an assault. It was a great tool for prying and breaking through barriers and doorways. Yet its wielder was shot through, but as he fell, Birback caught the haft of the axe and ran on with it like a Viking berserker. A Frenchman lifted his musket to parry a tremendous blow of the axe that descended for his head, but his parry was not enough. The large axe blade reached far over the parry and cleaved into his head. Birback went on to look for his next victim, quite content with his new weapon.

British troops began to pour over the parapet and formed up to fire a close volley before charging on after the hail of lead and into the smoke towards the French defenders. As Craven finished another off, he noticed the enemy were already starting to flee in the face of the terrifying advance of the 50th Foot. They were running towards a narrow doorway through a small building covered by the parapet of the outer line, where a narrow bridge led to the inner defence.

"Cut them off!"

Craven had realised what was happening. If the enemy could seal the door, they would render the inner defences secure. It would stall the assault entirely, perhaps giving them enough time to bolster the defences significantly. Hill had no more troops to bring up but the party that had traversed the mountains the night before. Charlie and Paget raced towards the door, being the nimblest amongst the unit, though Joze was not far behind. Charlie leapt into one using her entire bodyweight to launch the man aside, hacking down at him before he could get back to his feet. The rest of the British and French troops reached the doorway simultaneously, and a bloody hand-to-hand battle ensued with sword and bayonet. But a natural lull soon followed, as the attackers caught a breath and the French troops gathered together around their leader. Birback leapt into the doorway, almost blocking it off with his broad shoulders.

"Surrender!" Craven roared as a simple demand.

"I am Colonel Aubert, Commander of this garrison, and I will not," snarled the Frenchman proudly.

But a British Sergeant stepped up and thrust his spontoon through the proud Frenchmen, dropping him in one.

Paget looked a little upset by the affair, and yet the officer was fair game after the offer had been refused. Several of the British troops cheered in celebration, as the rest of the French troops before them laid their weapons down and gave up the fight. Craven rushed up to the inner defences to see the retreat for himself. The defenders of the bridgehead did not stay to defend it but fled across the bridge in panic.

General Hill soon reached the position with the rest of his force and got to see the sight for himself. The fleeing French troops were in complete disarray as they made their way to the Northern bank. Without the centre boats, they were forced to swim, with many drowning in the attempt. The guns of Fort Ragusa opened fire on Fort Napoleon, but the gunners of the Royal Artillery were already working to bring the captured guns into the fight. A single volley from Fort Napoleon smashed into the opposing smaller fort on the Northern bank, and the defenders had seen enough, fleeing for their lives.

Cheers rang out all the way along the lines as the assaulting force celebrated with great jubilation as General Hill took out his watch.

"Forty minutes, forty minutes and the bridge is ours," he said with delight.

The assaulters looked in remarkably good shape, as the blood action had been a short affair with so few casualties.

"I want that bridge restored immediately!"

"Sir?" Craven asked in surprise.

"We came here to destroy this bridge and all around it, and I will see the job done to completion, and leave nothing for the enemy. Restore that bridge so that we might march on over it and get to work over there before we finish the job for good," insisted Hill as he looked to the fort on the far side.

Several of the Highlanders stripped off their equipment and leapt into the river to swim across and retrieve some boats which might restore the centre of the pontoon bridge. They watched as the enemy formed up and marched away, not wanting any more part in the fight.

"Level these forts and thrown the guns into the river. Leave nothing for the enemy!" He turning to look South towards Miravete, "Only one obstacle remains," he declared.

They watched as French supplies and weapons were taken or discarded into the river. Soon enough, they were ordered to evacuate the fort as the bridge was set ablaze, and a great deal of powder placed in the two forts was set alight by slow match. Great explosions erupted and levelled both defensive structures. Yet as they formed up, a rider galloped up to General Hill.

"Sir, message from General Erskine, Sir!" cried the messenger.

Hill read it and sighed.

"What is it, Sir?" Craven asked.

"Soult marches with a relief force, and so denies us the final prize."

"Our work is done, more than done," insisted Craven as further explosions rang out in the distance.

"Yes, as much as was needed, but not all which could have been accomplished," he sighed.

"The job is done and with few casualties. I cannot imagine a better result."

Hill appreciated the sentiment.

"And you, what will you do now?"

"My orders are to cause chaos and uncertainty before I ride North."

"I imagine there is nothing you do better," smiled Hill.

"Yes, Sir, though have you not done the same here? This could have been remembered as several weeks of investment and bloody assault, successful or not, who might ever know, a most audacious raid, the sort that might make the likes of Colonel Trant blush."

Hill laughed.

"Thank you, Craven, and good luck to you."

"And to you, Sir."

He went back to the detachment of Salford Rifles he had brought with him. Despite a few bandages here and there, they had suffered no losses or severe wounds. It was a remarkable thing. Birback clung to the axe he had taken up during the battle, and it was still covered in the blood of those he had vanquished.

"Hanging on to that, are you?"

"It brought me luck."

Craven could not help but chuckle.

"On then, for we could not have hoped for a quicker triumph here, but our work is not done!"

CHAPTER 4

On the small party rode. Paget looked back and forth at the beautiful countryside with as much calm as he had upon their gentle ride before they crashed into Wellington and set their current whirlwind adventure in motion. He shook his head as he thought about the past few days.

"What is it?" Craven asked.

"It is Almaraz, Sir. In my head and in my heart, I was preparing for another Badajoz, or something like it, and yet here we are, done and moving on, as if it were nothing at all."

"Oh, it was something. Do not let the short time and few casualties deceive you. What was achieved there was nothing short of miraculous."

"Yes, Sir, and now? Where are we going. For it is most certainly not back from whence we came?"

"Into the wilds to meet an old friend," he smiled.

"Is it safe out here so far from the army, Sir?" Nooth asked from where he rode behind them.

"Safe?" Craven laughed, "Not at all. French scouts and raiding parties pass through these lands, as well as messengers who are now as well guarded as a general. Spanish Guerrillas fight back, but some of those might well take a chance against one of ours if there is some value to be had. The Bandidos are even worse."

"Then why do we come here?"

Nooth still felt like a complete stranger in an alien world after years of service in the militias in England, where they were celebrated by the locals and rarely saw violence of any sort.

"You assume we are any better!" Matthys replied.

Craven smirked and nodded in agreement until the sun was low in the sky once more, and they were forced to make camp. They soon got several small fires going but maintained sentries throughout. Nooth looked anxious at the prospect of a night in such a dangerous land, but that struck Craven as odd as he had served through worse since joining them.

"It's not this place that bothers him. It is what is in our future." Matthys had noticed Craven watching the man with concern.

"The mission we have here? It is little more than hit and run attacks."

"No, it is the great battle of our time which weighs on that man's mind, and on all of them. Everyone knew the day would come when Wellington had to engage with the main French army here in Spain."

"Have we not already?"

"No, and you know it. We have fought defensive actions; we have fought lightning assaults, and in every battle, we have fought with so many aspects in our favour. We have engaged the enemy whilst they were on the run, starving and disease ridden. We have fought them in the mountains with every advantage we could muster. But this time, in this year of 1812, we must engage the enemy in open battle."

"A fair fight, you mean?"

"In a way, yes. Wellington has a most wonderful military mind. For we have indeed survived here on this Peninsula because of it, but we have fought a defensive war ever since Talavera. Three years of fending off all the French could throw at us. But there is a great advantage in being the defender, and you know this."

"A defender chooses the ground, and has more time to react, and can see the enemy's opening plays."

"Yes, just like a duel," replied Matthys.

"But striking first can also have its strengths. Momentum, decisiveness, and terror."

"Terror? Did the weight of the French army bearing down on you strike fear into your heart, or did it temper it and make you stronger?"

Craven shrugged and sighed as he knew Matthys had a point.

"Then we are truly up against it?"

"Most definitely. Lord Wellington has made a name for himself as a defensive commander. We know that side of him and so does the enemy. He is cautious at all times and does not take risks, but none of us truly know how he will serve as we go forward."

"Does that not terrify you?" Craven was beginning to worry about it himself.

"The things I cannot change do not terrify nor concern

me. I only concern myself with what I can do, and what I can change, and how I can change the lives and destinies of those around me."

Craven took a long hard breath as he thought it over and finally smiled.

"I am with you," he replied, realising it was no different to a battle with cold steel. He mostly focused on what was at hand and within reach, and not what might be.

"He is right, you know," Charlie had been listening in from the sidelines.

"Really?" It was the last thing Craven would expect to hear from her, as she was always focused on the next battle, envisioning her next victims. She shrugged calmly.

"Go on, say it," insisted Matthys.

Craven looked confused, for he did not understand what was going on.

"Tell us why you fight," added Matthys.

"I put on this uniform so that I could kill Frenchmen. I was fuelled by anger and rage. I wanted nothing more than to tear them apart, without any regard for myself or anyone else. I was lost chasing revenge, always chasing revenge."

"And now?"

"Now I fight for those I love. I don't fight for me. I fight for us," she replied earnestly.

Craven was shocked by her outburst. Charlie's bloodlust was a constant in his life and had been since the fateful events surrounding the retreat to Corunna. She went on sounding more like the compassionate and thoughtful Matthys than the violent fanatic Craven had come to know in all this time.

"Carry those beside you to wherever the road leads, and

you will never be alone," she smiled.

The wind was taken out of Craven. He was stunned. He had not heard her speak so gently and lovingly for so many years, as if a great old friend had returned to his side.

"I was angry for a very long time, and I will carry that until the day that I die, but I will not be ruled by anger any longer. We must all focus on what is right before us, and all around us. We do not march to a battle with a French army, that is in our future. What matters is all that we do here and now. We can do good here, and we will, and so that when that future comes calling, we will be stronger, and we will be ready."

Paget had been listening, too, and a tear slid down his face as her words struck deep into his soul. Yet his eyes lit up as he came to a realisation.

"But you already knew that didn't you? Sir?" he asked Craven, who only smiled as he let him reach the conclusion himself.

"We ride to meet an old friend you say. We didn't come out here to fight this war alone."

"No," admitted Craven.

"Halt! Who goes there!" Moxy was on watch just twenty yards away.

"Right on cue," declared Craven as they watched several men step out from the shadows, unarmed and with a confident swagger.

"Rosa Mortal!" Paget gasped.

He recognised the confident, if arrogant prance of the Spanish militia leader who had fought Craven to a stalemate with blades and had done so much to help him recover from almost dying at the hands of Major Bouchard. The Spaniard wore a hugely wide brimmed hat with the hackles of three different French officers' headwear sewn onto it as literal triumphant feathers in his cap. He still wore his signature old style cup hilt rapier at his side, with as many pistols slung about his body as the infamous pirate Edward Teach. Yet his clothing was even more flamboyant than when they had last met, with more intricate embroidery and many French officers' silver buttons adorning his clothing. Many would call a man dressed such a way a peacock, but no one would dare say such a thing to Vicente Francisco De Rosas. Vicenta rushed forward upon seeing him and firmly embraced the man who was almost a father to her.

"We were not due to meet until tomorrow," declared Craven.

"When I receive a cryptic message apparently from Captain James Craven to meet at a place and time, I know it must be a challenge from the man himself or a trap set by his enemies or mine," smiled De Rosas, "I had to see for myself."

"Indeed," agreed Craven.

"So? Which is it?"

"I need your help, and it is Major Craven now."

De Rosas looked almost insulted before stepping closer to Craven, who reached subtly towards where he had always worn his dirk, forgetting it was there no more. Tensions were running high, but De Rosas stopped before Craven and placed a hand firmly on each of his shoulders.

"Finally, you are stepping up in life!"

He embraced Craven as closely as Vicenta had done. He laughed loudly before letting go and stepping back.

"I will help you, Major," he smiled, "And firstly, I shall

help by giving you a simple piece of advice. If you do not have a small blade within the reach of your hand, then you are not properly dressed!"

Craven shrugged.

"I had one, but it was broken."

But De Rosas looked down at the heavy coin purse hanging from his belt.

"And you could not afford a new one?"

"This money is to buy a blade, but not for me."

"I will sell you a blade. For that purse you may have my very own," he laughed as he looked down at his beloved rapier.

Craven doubted it was true, but De Rosas loved embracing the larger-than-life character which everyone knew him as.

"We really do need your help."

"The only help men come to me for is to fight battles for them."

Craven nodded in agreement.

"Major Craven came to me when he needed muscle, what an honour!"

He broke out into laughter once more and yet soon settled down as he realised Craven was not joking.

"Truly?"

"Yes."

"Go on."

Craven hesitated as he looked over De Rosas' shoulders to the men he had brought with him.

"Do you trust your soldiers here to hear what you have to say?" De Rosas asked.

"Yes, I do."

"Then you can trust mine. For if I could not trust them, I would never show them my back. These are men I trust with my life," declared the Spaniard firmly.

Craven looked to Matthys, questioning whether he should reveal the closely guarded secrets of Lord Wellington, but Matthys did not hesitate to nod in agreement, and so Craven continued.

"Wellington marches North to engage Marmont in open battle."

"Finally, then it has begun, the British campaign in Spain. I have waited years for this day to come. I never thought I would look forward to the day an Englishman marched into my country, but these are strange days and here we are."

"The two main armies that are a cause for concern for our army is Marmont in the North and Soult in the South. Wellington marches on Marmont, but he would have Soult believe he is the target also."

"And you think I can do this?"

"I know you can. Throw everything you have at the enemy and make them believe we are cutting a path South."

"My men work and fight every day. They do not lay about waiting for some task. How then could this be any different?"

"Because I will be there beside you. Let us strike hard and brazenly. Let us take risks and be bold, as if we had fifty thousand soldiers marching behind us to back our every play, and let the British redcoat be seen to be here and everywhere."

"I can do one better."

Craven was stunned and waited for him to explain further.

"The threat of British lines and cavalry is a powerful weapon, which I had already considered as a tool against the enemy. As we speak, there are men and women at work with the needle and thread."

"To what purpose?"

"So that British dragoons may ride through these parts and strike fear into the enemy."

"A deception? You would have your militia and guerrillas dress as British regulars? Do you know what kind of trouble that could bring down upon you?"

"Yes, and that is a weapon, too," smiled De Rosas.

Craven looked to Matthys to see he was equally as surprised, but also impressed, for they had a great tool at their disposal.

"Wellington asked me to oversee diversionary attacks so that the enemy believe he means to march South, or East, or North. Wellington would have the enemy in complete disarray, not knowing where our army is or where it will strike. He ordered me to create chaos, will you help me? Ride with us, and you may keep all the loot we find."

"All of it?" Birback protested.

"We cannot carry it anyway," replied Moxy.

"There will be more than you can imagine if we can defeat Marmont," insisted Ellis.

"There better be," growled Birback.

"I will help you, Major, and I will even fight for you, but I will not be led by you. I answer to no man," declared De Rosas as if he were a king.

"I never wanted to be a general."

"Good, but where is our Portuguese friend?" De Rosas was asking after Ferreira.

"Commanding the rest of our regiment under

Wellington."

"You left him idle whilst you do all the work? Indeed, you were not born to lead an army, for you should have sent him to do this," laughed De Rosas.

"I would see things done myself," replied Craven sternly.

"Yes, and I admire you for it, Captain…Major…" he stuttered before smiling.

"But you are right. I should put Ferreira to work," laughed Craven.

* * *

Ferreira was deep in conversation and laughter with his Portuguese comrades as they lovingly cleaned their rifles and swords to keep them not only in top service condition, but also as a matter of pride. He had been left the easy task just as Craven had said, but he heard the grunt of a horse and looked up. Two British officers were towering over them.

"Toiling like common muck," said one.

It was Colonel Blakeney and Major Rooke, the last men he would want to encounter. He'd rather face a dozen Frenchmen in deadly combat.

"It's called soldiering," he replied defiantly.

"How dare you speak to a superior officer with such a tongue!" Rooke cried.

"I would not, not to a superior man," he mumbled.

"What did you say?" Rooke demanded angrily.

Ferreira sighed with frustration and got to his feet. He took a deep breath before replying boldly so that there was no uncertainty.

"I said you are not a superior man."

Rooke looked disgusted as he turned to Blakeney for support, which only emboldened Ferreira further as his comrades watched on with glee.

"You have no authority over me, so what are you going to do? Demand satisfaction? Would you fight me with sword or pistol?" he demanded scathingly, knowing what the answer would be. The Caçadores behind him giggling only poured salt into the wound as Blakeney turned his nose up at them. Rooke remained silent but furious, and Ferreira kept moving forward as he let his anger burst out from deep within.

"Common muck you called me? Did you not? Calling a fellow officer and gentlemen common muck might cause such offence to many an officer that he might demand satisfaction. This rank and this uniform mean something to me, and I will fight and die to defend it. So, what will it be, Major? Will you retract your insult?"

"Calm down now, Captain. The Major meant nothing by it," insisted Blakeney.

"Then he will not mind apologising for the offence it caused if no ill will was intended." Ferreira calmly stuck firm in his defence.

Rooke looked deeply uncomfortable, but Blakeney smiled as he noticed Wellington passing casually by just a hundred yards away, and Ferreira spotted him, too.

"You will offer no challenge," snarled Blakeney as he gambled on Ferreira not taking any risks which might anger the General and bring disrepute to the uniform he claimed to wear so proudly, "You are common dago muck, and I will make sure you never forget it. Dogs like you and Craven have no place as commissioned officers, and it brings shame to us all. I will make it my mission to run you out of this army."

"My mission is to win this war, and an officer who does not understand that is a fool," snapped Ferreira.

Blakeney looked angry, but they had reached a stalemate. Neither would offer a challenge, nor could they take their complaints to Wellington. For he would not want to hear it, and it would only cause them all further trouble.

"This isn't over," hissed Blakeney before riding casually away with Rooke by his side.

"That took guts," declared Quental.

"And perhaps a little stupidity as well. Angering men like that will only bring more trouble."

"Yes, but perhaps it is better than placating them and suffering the same consequences anyway. Men like that have been shits their entire life, and the only way they will change is to become even bigger shits."

Ferreira chuckled, but as he watched the two despicable officers leave, he knew it would not be the last he would see of them. They had their sights firmly set on Craven and all who associated with him.

"That was a dangerous play," declared Gamboa, who having been raised up from the ranks was far more careful with how he spoke to fellow officers.

"I am finished with their nonsense. It is time someone spoke up."

"Like Mr Craven, Sir?" Gamboa asked.

"Yes, just like that."

"Is it not the Major's mouth that gets him in the most

trouble?"

Ferreira thought about it for a moment before shrugging, as if realising it was perhaps not the best course of action he had taken.

"Those bastards are coming after us no matter what. At least we can take a little joy in the discomfort we can bring them, and not lay down and have them trample all over us."

"Spoken like Major Craven himself," admitted Quental.

"Are you on his side or mine?" Ferreira asked as a friendly competitiveness still remained between them, for Gamboa was once a lowly Portuguese militia sergeant.

"I stand beside the Major and would follow him anywhere. It was not meant to insult, far from it. Perhaps we all need to be a little more like Major Craven."

"I am not sure you will find an officer in this army who would agree."

"Wellington would, begrudgingly perhaps, but he would," replied Quental.

Ferreira sighed in agreement. "Keep an eye out for those two. For they will not stop probing our defences."

"And yet they are powerless since General Le Marchant involved himself."

"Yes, if only we had more fighting officers and less talkers like those two," replied Ferreira as he watched the troublesome pair ride off into the distance.

CHAPTER 5

"If you want to attract the attention of the enemy, there is your target."

De Rosas pointed out ahead from the concealment of a hillside wood. Craven looked for himself with his spyglass and instantly shook his head. He was looking at a village that had been fortified into a complete defensive structure. The walls of the largest house had been extended to encompass four others and two barns by the use of palisades, a simple but effective measure. Inside, he could see at least fifty French soldiers on duty or wandering about, and there would surely be many more out of sight.

"A fort? You would have us attack a fort?" Craven gasped.

"Is that not what you came for?"

"Diversionary attacks and chaos, those are my orders."

"You want the enemy to believe that Wellington is about to march South. I do not attack this place because it would only attract the attention of a great many more enemies, but I am not trying to deceive the enemy, merely to kill them, and take from them. Whilst this place remains defended, there are a great many spoils to be had as supplies come and go."

"Why then would you want to destroy it?"

"I do not, not yet, but you do. We hunt and kill the enemy at every opportunity in these lands. We strike fear into their hearts and whittle away at them. But you, you want the French to believe that something has changed. Attack this place and you will ensure they believe it."

"I was thinking rather some smaller target."

But De Rosas merely looked back at him with a weary expression.

"What?"

"Captain Craven would jump at the chance of such an opportunity. What has happened in the time since last we met such that Major Craven lets his doubts and fears control him?"

Craven sighed. He was initially a little angry but then nodded in agreement with the assessment.

"I never wanted this promotion, but it meant a lot to those who follow me, but now that I have it, I cannot help but feel the importance of it weigh on me. I have a responsibility to them all in a way that I did not before, or not that I felt in the same way."

"You are looking at this all wrong. You are upside down, my friend."

Craven said nothing as he waited for an explanation.

"You do not need to change because of this promotion. You have been awarded it in recognition for what you were already doing, so do not stop being Captain Craven. The soldiers who follow you, they do not do it out of fear or for pay, but for love, for their love of you. Be the man they rewarded with this promotion."

Craven smiled, as he had forgotten how much he appreciated the Spaniard's wisdom.

"How is a man with your mind where you are? You should be a governor by now."

"For I would rather be king in a place where people want me to be, than ruling those who do not, and I think you are the same, Craven. You could have been commissioned into a most prestigious regiment by now. You could be earning more money and dining with lords and kings, but here you are, leading the same band of Bandidos you always have."

"Bandidos?" Craven grinned at the prospect of the Salford Rifles being addressed as such.

"It was as a compliment," added De Rosas.

Craven knew it and smiled.

"You are from a different time, Craven. You and I could just as well have been battling it out on the high seas in the Caribbean a hundred years past, or in the Roman arena, it would not matter. The times are changing, and eventually men like us will no longer be needed, but for now we are needed more than ever. This is not a time for parade soldiers, but for ferocious lunatics, just like me."

Craven agreed and felt a weight be lifted from his shoulders.

"So, then, what do you say?" De Rosas gestured towards the makeshift fort.

"Let's take it down," growled Craven.

"That's the spirit. I have long dreamed of the day I would ride with the great Captain Craven once more."

"Major," insisted Craven.

"Yes, just remember who is in charge."

"I surely do," laughed Craven.

"So, then, how shall we do this? Would you attack at night?"

Craven thought about it for a few moments before standing a little taller and shrugging off any doubts.

"No, we are the spearhead of fifty thousand soldiers and Wellington himself. We do not wait for nightfall. We do not approach with caution. We smash through the enemy as if they were nothing," he declared boldly.

"That certainly is the spirit!"

"They could have as many men down there as we do. This could be a bloody affair if we are not careful."

"Remember, you have the weight of Wellington's army behind you. Run over them."

Craven knew precisely what he meant, but it was easier said than done. They had to give the illusion of being a powerful rampaging force without actually being one.

"Do you have bugles?"

"Yes, we have taken many from the enemy. Some of my boys wear them as trophies, but we do not use them, for we do not want to make our presence known to the enemy."

"Today you do," smiled Craven.

"What have you got in mind?"

Craven did not reply as he carefully studied the fort and all of the terrain around it. De Rosas smiled as he could see the Captain who he knew so well was still inside, his tactical mind toiling away to find a solution to the problem before them.

"Come on, we have work to do."

He led the Spanish Commander back to their combined force. De Rosas had a little over fifty fighters at his disposal. It was hard to tell whether they were militia or guerrillas, their equipment was so mixed and ragtag, but they had a look of resilience and determination on their faces. Craven knew De Rosas would not command weak willed men, and so he was confident they would not run like the Spanish soldiers at Talavera, a scene which had marred the armies of Spain ever since. And not one Craven would forget soon. Despite his confidence in the fighters before him, nothing could change the fact that they had less than one hundred soldiers with which to attack a fortified position.

They eagerly awaited some news, but Craven did not know how to break it to them, but his mind soon wandered to the bridge of Almaraz and the assault that had taken the strong fortifications with such ease and so few casualties. He took a deep breath and finally came out with it.

"Over that ridge is a fort garrisoned by an enemy force at least as large as our own, perhaps larger still. On any other day I would stay well clear of such a place unless we had a sizeable force to make an attack, but De Rosas here believes I think too little of you all. He thinks you boys are more than up to the task."

Several of De Rosas' men translated for those who did not speak English, and they looked most disgruntled, as if they were ready to pick a fight with Craven for such an offence.

"It's working, isn't it?" he whispered to De Rosas.

"Of course. If you wanted them angry, you have achieved it."

"Do you have a plan?" Ellis asked with suspicion in his

voice.

Moxy looked surprised he had spoken out, as his quiet old friend rarely drew any attention to himself, and yet he seemed a different man since his past as an officer had been revealed.

"The enemy know two things. One, wherever they go they are attacked by militias, guerrillas and Bandidos," declared Craven.

"And the second?" Moxy asked.

"That in the confines of a well manned fort they are strong, for no ragtag rabble of Spaniards would dare risk going near them," smiled Craven.

"What are you saying?"

"That they feel safe where they are because nobody would be foolish enough to attack them," replied Ellis.

Craven pointed to him in agreement.

"But we…are stupid enough?"

"You are damned right we are, Moxy!"

"And that is a good thing?"

"We are going to attack that fort with overwhelming force, or at least the illusion of it."

"Yes, like Jemima Nicholas." Moxy remembered the trick they had used years before, just as the heroine Jemima had back in 1797.

"We can do this, if everyone does what is asked of them. Are you with me?"

Those who followed Craven did not question it further, but several of the Spaniards discussed it amongst themselves for a few moments. Finally, one of them spoke and addressed De Rosas directly.

"Do you believe in this plan?"

"I do," replied their Commander quickly without any doubt.

"Then, yes, tell us what we must do," replied the man as he addressed Craven.

"Wellington ordered me to create chaos, and that is precisely what we will do."

They all gathered around to hear the plan, and within twenty minutes they were in position and ready to begin. Craven had crept through the cover of a wooded area so that they were just two hundred yards from the fort but still concealed from the enemy. He had almost their entire force with him, but he peered over to the flank of the fort from his position to see Joze rush out from the cover of a tree. He ran towards the palisade with a bundle of dry kindling he had gathered together. He dumped it at the base of the palisade and took out an unloaded pistol which he would use to ignite a fire.

"Come on," whispered Craven as he watched the two sentries at the gate. It was large enough to ride a heavy cart through and the doors were open. The guards lay about without any care at all, much to Craven's relief. He watched as a wisp of smoke arose from the kindling, and Joze rushed on to a cart full of barley. It had been carelessly left outside of the palisade where it had been used to feed the horses of the garrison. Joze sparked another fire in the cart before putting his entire weight in against the cart and gave it everything he had until finally he managed to get it moving. He ran it towards the palisade, slowing the approach so as not to cause a violent crash. He ran the smouldering cart right up against the wooden wall.

"Yes, he did it," whispered Craven triumphantly.

"Now?"" De Rosas asked.

"No, not yet. Let the panic set in."

They watched for several minutes as the two fires began to build. They had gone unnoticed as Joze slipped away to the safety of the trees he had come from. The ground was bone dry and so were the wooden palisades, and it was not long before the fire spread as the entire barley filled cart went up in flames. The burning wood cracked and popped, and black smoke filled the air, wafting across the fortified position. It soon got the attention of several of the soldiers inside. Panicked calls echoed out as they rallied more men to help, yet the walls were already ablaze. They had their work cut out as the fires burned close to the houses they used to live in and store all their supplies. It was as hoped a scene of utter chaos.

"Now," he ordered to Moxy and Ellis who raised the last remaining Girardoni air rifles they had taken from the enemy. A marvel of technology that was near silent, and when in good working order a terrifying prospect. The two riflemen took aim and fired at the sentries on the main gate, striking them both down.

"Now!"

Craven leapt out from cover and ran on at a double-quick pace towards the open gates of the fort. They had covered half of the distance when an immense explosion erupted inside the defences. A powder store had gone up on flames. It shook the ground beneath their feet and caused all who closed on the fort to pause for a moment from the shock as dirt and debris was thrown up into the air.

"Was that all part of the plan?" De Rosas asked.

"No, it wasn't, but let's not waste this opportunity!"

Craven ran on, but their presence had been noticed as

several other sentries on the walls and a tower inside spotted their advance. A bell was violently rung, but many of the enemy clearly thought it was to call for aid to the fires as the garrison was in such a state of panic. An officer appeared in the main doorway to see for himself, but Craven shot him dead with his pistol and rushed on through without pausing. A number of the enemy were rushing to confront them whilst others continued to battle the flames.

"Form up!" Craven roared, "Three lines!"

He had a little over seventy muskets and rifles at his command. The first rank dropped to their knees whilst the other two took up staggered lines behind them.

"Present!"

A bristling line of muskets and rifles were directed at the enemy whilst they still struggled to form up.

"Fire!"

The volley was deadly and intoxicating as the cloud of powder smoke blended with the wood smoke, blinding them all. No more orders were given so as to not give away their intentions to the enemy, but everyone knew what they had to do, and they rushed forward with fixed bayonets and swords. They burst through the fog of powder and wood smoke and engaged the enemy just as they had recovered and were readying to fire, but it was too late. Craven's assault reached them, and cold steel clashed with few shots being released before the melee ensued.

A bugle blasted in the distance, and then another from further to the North.

"Cavalerie!" A panicked sentry cried out in fear and pointed out with both arms to different locations.

A French officer rushed up the ladder beside him to see for himself. He fixated on the positions as the bugles blasted out once more, and he caught a glimpse of blue-coated British light cavalry passing through the woods in the distance. He looked at a complete loss as he looked down at brutal melee below and then to the fires that would not be contained as they spread to the main house. Black woodsmoke swirled all about them. He said nothing as he rushed back down the ladder and fled for his life without a single word to those under his command. With his resolve also went the will to fight. Most of the French soldiers began to flee without any more resistance, and the rest soon followed as the defenders' willpower collapsed entirely. They ran for their lives with only what they had on their person, many hobbling away with injuries. Moxy hurried to load his rifle once more as they watched the enemy survivors run, which still numbered more than the force Craven had led.

"Leave them be," declared Craven.

"Why?" De Rosas asked.

"Because when they get to wherever they are going, I do not want them telling a tale of how they were cut down by a band of brutal savages almost to a man. No, I want them to tell a tale of how they were utterly overwhelmed by superior numbers," smiled Craven.

The gunfire came to an end, but the fires continued to rage at their backs as there was no one battling them any longer. Cheers rang from the assaulters who could barely believe what they had achieved.

"Casualties?" Craven asked Matthys, who was already seeing to one of the injured.

"Eight wounded, none killed," he replied proudly and in

appreciation of Craven's interest in the wellbeing of them all.

"Now that is the work of the Captain Craven I knew," declared De Rosas as the so-called cavalry raced up behind them, still blasting their bugle horns as if they were leading an entire squadron. Craven watched with glee as the enemy fled as quickly as they could, surely taking the news of their downfall to the next safe location down the road.

"It's going to work, I am certain of it," whispered Craven to himself.

CHAPTER 6

Ferreira roared his orders in English as he drilled the Salford Rifles. There were more Portuguese amongst them than British, which now gave him a sense of pride which he never used to feel. Most wore the British redcoat, except those Caçadores he had brought with him, but that didn't matter, for they fought as one. They marched on through the hot sun, but it did not feel like hard work, for they knew that their efforts were paying off. They had driven the French from Portugal, besides some minor skirmishes across the border in the North, and it felt like they would soon drive the French all the way back to France, where they would finally feel truly safe once more, with an allied Spain as the buffer they once were.

"I hear the supplies for the army are thin," said Quental as he rode beside Ferreira.

"Yes, the French are attempting to do what we have long done to them. Starve them of food, powder, their communications."

"And wine."

"Ferreira turned to him in surprise as if he knew something more.

"I hear Lord Wellington's personal supply column was attacked and that the wine and Madeira for most of the senior staff was taken."

Ferreira did not seem to delight in the fact and looked more concerned than anything else.

"What is it?"

"I march the men to rendezvous with wagons sent by the Lady Sarmento. Food and wine and all the luxuries fit for a king."

"You think they might have been targeted?"

"This far North it is a possibility."

"How long until we reach them?"

"Not far now. We cannot march back into camp without such a wealth of resources if they are indeed still ours to collect."

"Then do not return. The boys are quite happy to spend a night out here, for we have spent half of our days doing so it feels."

"Not returning to the army so that we may get drunk whilst the staff of this army go thirsty?"

"Why not?"

"Why not indeed?" Ferreira smiled mischievously.

But doubt began to creep into his mind that their supplies would have made it past the French attacks, but they marched on. Soon enough to their delight they came into view of several wagons stopped beside a small stream. They were gathering water for man and beast as well as taking a much-needed rest.

"Is that it? Is that ours?"

"It is!" Ferreira roared excitedly as he dug in his heels and galloped forward, leaving those on foot in the dust and Quental hurrying to keep up. The wagon drivers recognised them and waved as they approached. They were not soldiers, and yet they were well armed with muskets, pistols, and swords with which to protect their valuable cargo.

Ferreira leapt from his horse and jumped up onto the back of one of the open wagons to see for himself what the Lady has sent for them.

"Puta merda," he declared in astonishment at the treasures he was now beholding.

"Captain!" Quental bellowed.

There was concern in his voice, and so Ferreira reacted quickly and followed Quental's gaze. A party of more than a dozen horsemen were approaching, and at the head of them was Colonel Blakeney. The party was only partially in uniform and were in fact dressed and equipped for the hunt. Ferreira sighed as he knew this meant trouble. Blakeney led his party right up to them as he looked about in surprise at the well laden carts.

"What is it you have there, Ferreira?" Blakeney demanded, who had brought many more officers along for the ride from other regiments.

Ferreira knew he could not lie, for he would soon be caught in it, and also that he had to appear civil before the other officers of Blakeney's party.

"Wine and other gifts sent from the Lady Sarmento, Sir, to Major Craven and the Salford Rifles."

"Wine? You will know a great deal of wine and other sundries were taken by the enemy on this very road, including those meant for Lord Wellington himself."

"Yes, Sir."

"Are you sure all of this was sent for you? The provosts would not take kindly to supplies to the army being stolen."

"I am very certain, Sir, and the men driving these wagons can attest to it," growled Ferreira.

He thought he had saved the situation, but Blakeney merely smiled and changed tactics.

"Would you have your army's Commander and his staff go thirsty whilst you can replace what the enemy have taken?"

Ferreira groaned as he could see where the situation was heading.

"The men of the Salfords getting merry on a great horde of wine whilst Lord Wellington has an empty cup might not endear many to you, Captain, and what a great gift it would be to Lord Wellington in these hard times."

The officers about him cheered and showed their support for the idea.

"Well, Captain? What will it be? I will be glad to escort these wagons to Lord Wellington personally and ensure no harm comes to them."

Ferreira hesitated, looking to Quental for help, but he knew there was nothing to be done. He was at risk of looking like both an ungrateful fool and perhaps even a thief if he did not agree. Few would believe that such a rich haul was sent to a lowly infantry Major and the small body of soldiers under his command. Blakeney leapt from his horse and climbed up onto the same wagon as Ferreira as if they were close friends. It was all an act for his audience, but it was working. He eyes lit up in disbelief at the riches which he lay his eyes upon.

"Lord Wellington will greatly appreciate this gift, and it will well replace those supplies which were so unfortunately lost. Thank you, Captain, and you must thank Major Craven."

Ferreira looked at a loss as the rest of their column approached. They were so close to getting what was rightly theirs, and yet so far. Ferreira climbed down from the wagon.

"Give my regards to Lord Wellington, Sir, and ensure these gifts from Major Craven and the Salford Rifles are received in good order," he replied begrudgingly.

In just a few moments the wagons were back on the road and under the escort of Blakeney and his friends. The despicable Colonel waved his hat back at them as they rode away. To the officers of his hunting party, they would surely take it as a gesture of good will, but Ferreira knew it was very much the opposite as Blakeney rubbed it well and truly in their noses.

"Wellington will never see those supplies, will he?" Quental asked.

"I highly doubt it," admitted Ferreira.

"You had no choice. If you had tried to hang onto those wagons, the best-case scenario is we would look like greedy fools, and worst case could have been very bad indeed."

Gamboa brought the column to a halt and approached alone.

"They took everything?"

"You would not believe the delights that were on those wagons," lamented Ferreira.

"Nobody crosses Craven for long and gets away with it. He will pay for this," seethed Quental.

* * *

"Ready?" Craven asked.

"Ready," replied De Rosas.

They rose up from a small embankment with rifles and muskets at the ready and took aim at a column of French cavalry scouts.

"Fire!" Craven ordered.

The crack of a great volley erupted, and smoke wafted over them, knocking many from their horses. But as the cloud of powder smoke was swept away by the winds, the enemy Cavalry were looking to engage. Yet trumpets blasted out once more from further down the valley as a stream of two-dozen British light cavalry came galloping towards them. The French cavalry quickly turned tail and fled as rifle fire followed them. Cheers followed the gunfire.

"Another triumph, you certainly are going to draw attention to this place," declared De Rosas.

"I hope we don't bring too much trouble to your door." Craven was genuinely concerned.

"So long as your Lord Wellington engages with Marmont's army, it will all be worth it."

Craven sighed.

"I do not have control over what Wellington does, but I can assure you that he will do everything in his power to face the enemy in open battle."

"He must, for I am sad to say that the armies of my country cannot stand against the French. There was a time when we were the greatest soldiers in the world."

"You are fighting against the might of Napoleon and his Empire. I have seen the fighting spirit in your people. I saw it today, and I have seen it often. You need us, the army of Portugal and Spain, but never forget that we need you, too. Without the resistance of the men and women of Spain, we would have no hope of continuing this war, let alone winning it."

"As an Englishman, I imagined you would believe you could do it alone."

"No, Napoleon chased us out of Spain once, and we did not even stand to fight against him. None of us are strong enough alone, but together, I believe we can be. A clever Spaniard once taught me that," smiled Craven.

De Rosas thought fondly back upon the memories of how he dragged Craven out of the emotional pit of despair he had once been cast into by Major Bouchard.

"My country has been at war for so long now I sometimes wonder how hope can remain, and yet I think back to those days. I watched you come back stronger than you ever had been, and that gives me hope."

"Craven defeated Bouchard, Sir, without any tricks and before us all in the ruins of Ciudad Rodrigo. I watched the Major defeat that villain one on one in a fair fight," Paget blurted out.

"He is dead, then?"

"He ran with his tail between his legs," beamed Craven.

"Then you should have shot him in the back," seethed De Rosas.

"Where is the honour in that?" Paget asked.

"There is no question of honour with a man like that. He has plundered, raped, and murdered his way across my country, and every day he draws breath he does more damage. He deserves no respect. The next time you see that man you do not show him mercy, will you promise me?" De Rosas asked Craven.

"After all you have said to me, you would have it come to that?"

"This war is not a game for us. I thought there was some nobility in it, but I was wrong, especially when it comes to murderers like Bouchard. Promise me you will not hesitate to end him again?"

"You have my word."

Paget was a little rattled by the prospect, for such murderous intent no matter the circumstances of a meeting was repulsive to him. But when he looked to Charlie for some understanding she only nodded in agreement with De Rosas' request. Even this new mellower version of Charlie could not stand for Bouchard to go on living.

"What makes you think we will see him again?" Paget asked, hoping to avoid such an eventuality.

"You will, for a grudge like this does not end until one or both is killed," insisted De Rosas.

"And if one of us gets the chance at him?"

"You pierce his heart and be sure that he is dead," growled De Rosas.

Paget looked deeply uncomfortable once again and looked to Craven for some assistance.

"Can we do that, Sir? As officers of His Majesty's army?"

"Nobody would question it," admitted Craven.

"Perhaps not, but should we with good conscience?"

De Rosas was disgusted that the question even needed to be answered as Craven mulled it over and finally came up with his answer.

"I have seen my contest with Bouchard as a feud between

two men, but it is more than that," he replied as all of the detachment he had with him gathered around. Their celebrations had faded away now as they listened in to the debate. Craven went on.

"Major Bouchard is a threat to all the people of Spain. He is not to be treated with the respect of a soldier or an officer. From now on, if any one of you gets a chance at that bastard you take it, do you hear me?"

Most of them were stunned.

"Should he not pay for his crimes in a court?" Paget asked.

"No," snapped Craven.

"There is no good in that man. End him and let the Lord judge that devil as he sees fit," declared Matthys boldly.

None of them had ever known Matthys to call for the death of a man, and it struck them deep to the core. Craven took out the purse of money Le Marchant had given him to purchase a sword.

"This coin purchase goes to the one who makes the kill, and if it is by my hand, I will spend it on the grand celebration with all the food and drink you can imagine. What do you say, will you do it?"

"You are asking for a death warrant? Do you know that, Sir?"

"Yes, I do, because De Rosas is right. Every day Bouchard lives he ruins more lives. I don't care if you shoot him from five hundred yards or if you slit his throat while he sleeps. Bouchard dies, do you hear me?" Craven demanded solemnly.

"You let him live, Sir, when he lay sick in bed," replied Paget.

"And that was a mistake. I let him live because of my own

pride, and how many lives has he taken because of it? There is no honour in fighting Bouchard, but his death will save many."

Paget still felt deeply uncomfortable, but he would not resist any further.

"Major Craven!" a voice called out from one of their party.

He was directed down to the bodies of the French dead, of which Birback and several of the Portuguese fighters were already looting, but that was not what his attention was being drawn to. He noticed a man pointing towards a lone French cavalryman who was approaching slowly and without any threat. He had no weapons in his hands, only a thin tree branch with a white flag atop it, asking for a peaceful meeting.

"It could be a trick," declared Matthys as he hurried to reload his rifle and many of the others did likewise.

"What shall we do, Sir?" Paget asked.

"You should not be seen, for we would not have the enemy know that you are here."

"Why? Would it not strike fear into them?"

"We do not know how they would respond, and that is the problem. Our job is to cause confusion and make the enemy believe the army advances this way, but you are known for your deceptions," replied Matthys to Craven.

"Deceptions?"

"You have Spanish guerrillas dressed as British cavalrymen."

Craven shrugged as he knew he had no defence.

"I will handle this."

Matthys set out over the ledge before anyone could stop him, yet they took up positions and waited with weapons at the ready should they be needed. Matthys shouldered his rifle and went on to meet with the cavalryman, stopping almost ten yards short so that he would have time to take up his rifle or sword to defend himself in the case of foul play.

"What do you want?"

The cavalryman was an officer and looked most inquisitive as he studied every element of Matthys before speaking a word, a trait Matthys would normally respect, but in this case, it concerned him. For he was not dealing with any common soldier. Finally, he spoke.

"You are Sergeant Matthys of the Salford Rifles?"

Matthys was most unnerved, as there was no good reason why the Frenchman should have such information.

"Who is asking?" Matthys demanded angrily.

"I have a message for Major Craven," declared the officer before casting a leather satchel out into the ground between them. The Frenchman said nothing more as he turned and led his horse away calmly and with no urgency.

Matthys approached the bag with suspicion. He drew out his sword and poked at it as if he expected some elaborate trap. But as he did so, Craven and several others came down to hear the news for themselves. Craven grabbed the bag without any concern at all and ripped it open, taking out a small, folded piece of paper. Matthys was stunned, but also curious.

"What does it say?"

"It's addressed to Major Craven. It says to come and meet at the location below at noon tomorrow. It's signed Colonel Mizon."

"Mizon?" Matthys asked in horror.

None of them had seen him since Fuentes de Oñoro where the French Colonel had almost cost them Craven's brother Hawkshaw. And in turn Craven killed the French officer's savage henchman Braun who had made the attempt on Hawkshaw's life. Nobody said a word as they considered what this meant.

"If he knows you are here that is not good," declared Matthys.

"And he knows of your promotion?" added Paget.

"He may know nothing, and this is one of many attempts to finding out if you are out here?" Ellis suggested.

"It might not even be him, who can say?" Moxy joined in.

But Craven shook his head as it all felt too convenient.

"He knew who I was. He named me by rank, name and regiment," added Matthys.

"Then whoever this comes from they know I am here, and that can only be Mizon or Bouchard."

"What will you do, Sir?" Paget asked.

"This could be a chance to strike down an important Frenchman here on Spanish soil," insisted De Rosas.

"Or a trap, which I find far more likely," replied Matthys.

"What could either of those Frenchmen have to say to me?"

"Nothing, for they both want you dead," added Ellis.

"Gather anything worth taking. I won't stay here a moment longer than we need to," declared Craven, realising how compromised they were and potentially dangerous the situation could be. They all went to work quickly except those in command who stayed with Craven.

"You are a popular man," smiled De Rosas.

"If this is real, and Mizon knows I am here, then you are all in danger," replied Craven with genuine concern.

De Rosas smiled as he put a hand on Craven's shoulder.

"My dear, Captain…I mean, Major…we have been in danger long before you ever walked into our lives, and any danger you have brought upon us is most welcome."

"Why?"

"Because whatever battles you fight are also our battles. I don't know why every Englishmen is here in Spain, but I think it is mostly for pay and plunder, but not you."

"That is exactly why I came here. I came to make my fortune in a war where there was the potential to make it," replied Craven in despair.

But De Rosas' did not even look surprised by the apparent revelation.

"Now what do you see? Do you see a hero which they think they see?" Craven looked to those who followed him.

"I do, indeed."

Craven sighed with exhaustion. "How can you still believe in me?"

"I am not sure you understand Spain at all, James. We are a country built on passion, and you have gone from a selfish man to a hero to which so many look up to. You are what we would all aspire to be. You are a man of passion who is not afraid to show it, no matter the cost. The men I command, they look to you as a hero, because you do not fight for pay, but for passion."

"I am not sure that is true."

"But I am. Are you a wealthy man?"

"No," replied Craven who had little to his name but what he carried.

"In all these years you could have made yourself a rich

man, I am sure of it, but you have not."

"Not through want of trying, I assure you," sighed Craven.

"I do not doubt that you want it, but I know there are things you want more. You are different from the rest, Craven, and my men see it. And so do yours."

"I hope it doesn't cost them their lives."

"My point exactly," smiled De Rosas.

"You have led men, so tell me, what should I do?"

"If this is indeed Mizon, then he means to undermine you, and if it is not, then it is a trap."

"Either way it is a trap, then?"

"Yes."

"Then what should I do?"

"Trust your instincts, and trust those who have had your back throughout."

They moved out to a place of safety as they all contemplated what Mizon's return could mean, and what he could want. There was no celebration of their successes about the fire that night, but plenty of discussion as many speculated on what the next day would bring.

"Do you believe Mizon really knew it was you? Perhaps he sent out many similar messages scattered all about the land in the hope that he might find you, rather than having any true knowledge you were here?" Paget asked who was more curious than any of them.

"Even if that that is true, the messenger recognised Matthys, and so he knows now for certain."

"If it even is the Colonel, anyone could have written that note, Sir."

"No one would be foolish enough to impersonate that

man, and nobody would want to."

"If you are so certain it is him, then what does he want?"

"What he always wants, victory for France at any cost," replied Matthys.

"But what does he want with Major Craven?"

"To see him dead, I should imagine."

"Perhaps but let him play his hand."

"And if that is an attempt on your life? It would not be the first time."

"Then we will be ready for it."

"We have seventy men, and you will meet at a time and place of his choosing. He could have a whole army waiting for you," protested Matthys.

Craven smiled.

"What is so funny, Sir?"

"That you two think he can muster an army. The French are spread thin. They still try and keep control of this whole country, and so they spread their armies far and wide, with little in between to keep them stitched together, all the while soldiers like us and the guerrillas and partisans gnaw away at them. No, he does not bring an army, but he will try to find a way to take me out of this fight. Of that much I am certain."

"Then you should not go, Sir."

"Of course, he should," roared De Rosas.

"But it is a trap. He must surely not go."

"Perhaps, but a man like Craven does not back down. He does not hide from the enemy."

Paget looked anxious.

"Please, Sir, do not risk your life for the sake of pride," he pleaded.

"There are worse things a man can risk his life for, many of them," replied De Rosas.

But Paget looked flustered.

"We could set our own trap and catch that bastard?" Charlie suggested.

But Craven shook his head.

"The white flag was flown, and I am bound to comply with respect, and I will do it. For if I do not, then it has no meaning. How can we ever expect it to have meaning if we do not respect it here and now?"

"But Mizon will not, Sir," replied Paget.

"Bouchard would not, but Mizon, he is our enemy, but a very different kind."

"At least let us ride out and cover you throughout and be ready for the trap," pleaded Paget.

"Most certainly. I will go in peace, but I am not a fool."

Paget breathed a sigh of relief, but it was not all he had hoped, and he looked into the fire deep in thought.

"We will be there, don't worry," Charlie tried to reassure him.

CHAPTER 7

Craven stopped his horse and looked out into the open ground beyond. They were still well concealed by a wood. It was a large level area of elevated ground, with no natural features towering over it where a sharpshooter might see out. He took out the note that the French cavalryman had delivered to him and read it again before double-checking his map. The landscape was barren. For it was once a farmer's crop, but nothing had grown on it this year, and there were signs the field had been set ablaze not long ago.

"That is the spot," he finally declared and pointed to a spot out in the open. There was no sign of any French presence, but Craven checked his watch to find they were an hour early, just as he wanted to be.

"I don't like it, Sir," declared Paget.

"Noted," replied Craven.

"Have they not arrived yet or are they hidden? That is the

question," replied Matthys.

"French soldiers do not attempt to hide in my country, for they are soon discovered. The people who live across these lands ensure that they are discovered, and so the French, they either stay in their strongholds or they stay moving," replied De Rosas.

"Then they are not here yet," replied Craven.

"Or they encircle us as we sit here helpless," replied Paget in concern.

"We are hardly helpless," laughed Craven.

But Paget would not hear it, and he had his long rifle resting across the saddle ready to use at a moment's notice. Craven leapt from his saddle and tied his horse up to a tree. He then sat down against another tree where he had a clear view of the meeting place.

"This is it? We are going to wait here?" The enemy could be encircling us while we sit here idle," complained Paget.

"Let us not presume to know what our enemy is doing, but the danger is no different than any other day we are out here," replied Matthys.

"Any Frenchman who dares do us harm will be shot dead before he can try," declared Moxy as he marvelled at the clear view in all directions. He felt confident and safe, knowing he could hit a target further out than any other man, and the French made no official use of rifles. For Napoleon himself despised the slow rate of fire.

"Look at it, a clear view for miles," declared Moxy, "At this distance we could loose off two shots against cavalry and many more against those on foot. It would take a great force to endanger us."

"Yes, and Mizon knows that, too, which is what worries

me."

"You think he is lulling us into a false sense of security?"

"It is what I would do, Sir," replied Paget.

"Even if that were true, he would have to back it up. Moxy is right. It would require hundreds of soldiers to advance on us here with any success."

"Or wait us out, for we have no supplies," replied Paget.

"Impossible, for it would take thousands of soldiers in a great perimeter to stop us slipping away," replied Craven.

"Then you believe the Colonel is honest and upfront about this?"

"Not a chance," laughed Craven, "Mizon does not do anything lightly, and he has a sharp mind. He wants something from us. I am just not sure what."

Paget groaned with frustration as he was not comfortable with the situation at all.

"It is okay. We are okay," insisted Charlie.

The wait felt like a whole day, but finally, there was movement far off into the distance.

"Sir!" Paget shot to his feet with his spyglass.

Craven was drowsy as he dipped in and out of sleep in the warm late morning sun. He slowly got up to see for himself, but without the excitement and rush exhibited by Paget.

"Well?"

"It is him, Sir," replied Paget before Craven got a good look himself.

"Almost in range," declared Moxy.

"That is not Bouchard," insisted Craven.

"But he needs to die."

"Very much so, but not under a white flag," declared

Craven who noticed the same officer who had delivered the message to them riding beside the Colonel and carrying the same flag.

"You will respect that flag. But will he, Sir?"

Craven did not reply as he watched the French force come into view far across the open plain. Mizon was supported by two-dozen horsemen but seemingly no more. They came to a halt outside of Moxy's range, ostensively knowing the limitation and their position, and that only worried Paget further. The French Colonel took the white flag from the other man and rode on alone.

"Six hundred yards, with little wind, I could do it," declared Moxy.

"And if he shows any sign of trouble, you will take that shot, but not before, is that clear?" Craven ordered.

"Yes," replied Moxy in disappointment as Craven mounted up onto his horse.

It was a tense moment as none of them wanted to see Craven go out alone.

"Stay sharp, but not just on Mizon. Do not be distracted by whatever this is. Keep eyes all about and be ready for anything," he ordered.

"Sir, it could still be a trap. The ground looks empty from here, but we do not know what preparations the enemy have made. They could have many soldiers hidden from our sight. You think you are going to meet one soldier and it could be many."

"Be vigilant," ordered Craven as he shrugged off the concerns and rode on.

He was fully armed but empty-handed, as all he carried

was sheathed and holstered, with his rifle resting across his back. Soon enough he was well out of earshot of his comrades and began to wonder if he had made the right decision, yet he showed no fear. Mizon had stopped a few hundred yards away from his escort and likely well out of their reach should he need them. Mizon was all alone and appeared to be relying on the white flag to protect him. Craven stopped ten yards short of the Frenchman, close enough that they could speak, but with enough room that he had time to react if any tricks were pulled on him. Once his horse had come to a standstill, he realised just how quiet and peaceful the open plain was, for there was not even a gentle breeze. Everything was calm and still, just as Mizon was until he lowered the banner to rest it across his saddle now that their meeting had begun.

For a few moments each man weighed the other up and said nothing, but it was the glistening of the sun from the hilt of Mizon's sword which drew his attention. To Craven's surprise the hilt was identical to his own, the regulation of a British infantry officer. However, the hilt of Mizon's sword was made in solid silver, which is why it glistened so brightly. Whereas his own sword had once had gilt covering all its bronze components, but much of that had been worn away in the hard years of service.

"Beautiful, isn't it?"

Mizon followed his gaze to the weapon which was sheathed in an elaborately engraved leather scabbard with matching silver fittings.

Paget watched anxiously as the French Colonel casually drew out his sword.

"Be ready to fire," he ordered Moxy.

It would be a very long-distance shot, and at such extreme distances there was a risk of striking Craven, too. But Moxy was not bothered, for he believed in his own abilities, and nobody would doubt him.

"Easy now, no man ever struck a blow from ten yards," declared Matthys.

"Have you never thrown a sword?" De Rosas asked.

"No, I haven't," replied Matthys in surprise.

De Rosas sighed with amusement.

Craven admired the gleaming sword from afar. The blade was much older than the hilt and not of British origin, just as was the case with his own beloved sword, as if the French Colonel was copying his style.

"I took this sword from an enemy, or from two in fact. The hilt is of the finest of craftsmanship from London and the blade, an old Toledo one, from when Spain's star shone so great."

Craven much coveted the sword, but not for himself. For he knew it would make a fine gift to General Le Marchant and perfectly fit his requirements. Mizon was enjoying his envy as he sheathed the sword once more and remained silent. He seemed to revel in Craven's confusion as to why he had even been summoned.

"Congratulations on your promotion, twice over," declared Mizon.

So, he knew about Craven's demotion and quick promotion which followed, too. That was of concern, but he tried to not show it as the Frenchman tried every trick to unnerve him.

"What do you care?"

"I care a great deal, for I know talent when I see it."

Craven was stunned as he was expecting to have to be on the defensive, but he then became suspicious.

"What do you want, Colonel?"

"I want you. France is winning this war, and no amount of small victories Wellington can achieve with cheap tricks will change that. Soon enough, your army will meet with ours and it will be defeated. Even if it is not, it will be defeated by the next French army, or the one after that. I am sure you know that Napoleon prepares the greatest army ever seen. They say he has one million soldiers at his disposal. One million, can you believe it? What can your Lord Wellington do against such a force?"

Craven shrugged as if he did not care, but the truth was it was a horrifying prospect. He knew what Napoleon was capable of with just tens of thousands, let alone an army the size of some countries. Craven had no words, but Mizon went on.

"France has great armies and great leaders, but good fighting men are always to be needed. Men who can inspire. Major, you came here to make yourself a rich man, but it seems you are no closer to that ambition than when you started out. Join us. Fight for France, and I will make you a rich man, but more so than that, you will be a rich man on the winning side. For make no mistake, we will win this war. Would you be a rich winner or a poor loser?"

Craven had heard it all before, and it was not even the first time Mizon had tried to buy him.

"I will never fight for France," he growled.

"But you will fight for Spain? You will spearhead an advance for officers who care nothing for you? Marshal Soult knows your intentions and he will be ready."

"You know nothing of our plans," cursed Craven angrily.

"Soult is not Wellington's target at all, is he?" replied Mizon with a smirk.

Craven had let passion get the better of him. He had given so little away, and yet it was enough for the razor-sharp and clever Mizon to pick up upon.

"So, Wellington marches North to Marmont. Thank you Major," he smiled.

Craven bared his teeth angrily, but he was angrier with himself for letting the information slip. He considered what he would say, and yet he knew there was no refuting it now. Mizon had gleaned what he wanted from Craven, and it was too late to change that.

"Always a pleasure, Craven."

Mizon turned and rode away. Craven was furious as he turned back and galloped back to his comrades who were most surprised that no battle nor surprise attack had broken out.

"What does he want, Sir?" Paget shouted as Craven approached.

"He knows Wellington marches North, and he knows our work here is nothing more than diversionary!"

"You told him?" Moxy asked in disbelief.

"I didn't have to, but he got it out of me anyway," replied Craven angrily.

"What do you want to do?" Matthys asked.

"Let us go after him and hunt him down. We can still catch him, Sir!" Paget leapt up onto Augustus to prepare for a pursuit.

"No!" Craven snapped.

Paget froze.

"He may not be able to put us in danger here, but we

would be fools to ride right into whatever trap awaits us over there," explained Matthys.

Craven nodded in agreement. It was precisely what he was thinking even though he could not find the words to express it. He was still seething with rage at himself.

"What will you do?" De Rosas asked.

"Our time here is done."

"Mizon only speculates. We could continue our work, Sir. His superiors may not believe the Colonel if we continue what we have been doing here."

"Mizon knows, and the fact is it is true. And the more time that passes the more evidence he will have, and the more weight his information will carry. We never intended to stay here for good. We did what we came here to do, but our place is with the army now."

"Finally, Wellington will march out and engage the main French army in open battle?" De Rosas asked with glee after Craven had promised to ensure it would happen.

"Yes, and we will be there when the two armies clash."

"Then I suppose this is goodbye once again?"

"I am afraid so."

De Rosas was clearly saddened by the news, but he also respected it. He drew out a large, sheathed knife from his belt and walked up to Craven, offering it up to him whilst he remained in the saddle.

"To replace the one you have lost."

Craven took the blade which was ornate and elaborate. It had the distinctive canted grip which so many Spanish knives did. It was clearly his own and deeply treasured, and that meant a lot to Craven who greatly valued a personal blade. It was a large, fixed blade which was really too long to be used for utility. It was a fighting weapon through and through.

"That blade was forged by my uncle, who is sadly no longer with us. It will never fail. It is unbreakable, and as such represents the bond between us."

"Between your uncle and yourself?"

"No, between you and I."

Craven was stunned into silence.

"I do not gift this to you. I only permit you to carry it until this war is done, and when it is, you will return it to me. Is that clear?"

"Of course," replied Craven, realising the weapon meant more to the Spaniard than any he had ever personally owned. For a family connection was not something he could ever have had.

"No man may carry this blade but my blood, but you are my brother, and he would have liked you. Wear it with pride, fight with passion, and when the fighting is done, wield it no more!"

"You have my word." Craven thrust it deep into his officer's sash where his own dirk had once resided until it met its end.

"Mount up!" Craven roared as his detachment of the Salford Rifles prepared to depart.

"Sir, why did Mizon draw out his sword?" Paget could not help but wonder at his action.

"To boast of it."

"Is it a fine weapon, Sir?"

"One fit for a general," Craven grinned back at him.

It took Paget a few moments to understand what he

meant, but when he did, he could not help but agree. He was not comfortable to taking Le Marchant's coin purse for themselves, but it was hard to deny that the sword carried by an adversary such as Mizon would make a fine gift indeed.

"Thank you for all that you have done," said De Rosas as they prepared to depart.

"No, thank you, for we have achieved more together than either one of us could have alone, and whilst England and Spain and Portugal remain united, Napoleon will not win. But they say he has amassed a great army in France, some say it is a million strong. I suspect that is an exaggeration, but if it is half that number, then it should be a great worry to us all."

"Does he not march to Russia?"

Craven looked impressed that a Spanish guerrilla leader would be so well informed.

"That is the rumour. For the Russians sent him an ultimatum, and is there a world in which issuing such to a man like Napoleon would result in anything but war?"

"Then they expect it and are ready for him?"

"I don't think anyone is ever ready for an army led by that man. Just be glad he left Spain to others."

"We cannot run and hide from him forever," insisted De Rosas.

"No, we cannot."

"And, Craven?"

"Yes?"

"Amalia, she asks after you whenever our paths cross. Do not forget her."

"That would be impossible," he smiled before turning his horse about and leading his party North.

Despite the shock meeting with Mizon, they went on in good spirits, for the ride North is what they had all been waiting for with great anticipation.

"Then the time has finally come? We march on to engage Marmont, Sir?" asked Paget.

"We do."

"Then perhaps we may strike before Colonel Mizon can carry his news to Marshal Soult?"

"Soult may not even believe him, and the roads are perilous. The enemy have a great difficulty in receiving communications as they are hindered at every turn. All of Spain is hostile to them. A whole country working against their forces, whilst we move with ease and the assistance of the people," added Matthys as he brought some hope.

"None of it matters now. We did what we came to do. We must reunite with Wellington's army with all haste and hope they have not fought and won the battle without us!" Craven cried excitedly.

"Huzzah!" Paget roared.

CHAPTER 8

Two days hard riding, and they knew they must be close to the army. But to Craven's surprise the first sign of the army was not the cavalry scouts which skirted the army, but Timmerman and his band of rogues as they converged on one road and came alongside one another.

"You march to fight Marmont?" Craven asked in disbelief.

"I wouldn't miss it for the world, and we are in this together, are we not?"

"Well, yes, but I wasn't sure you ever realised it," smiled Craven.

"I never thought we'd ever bury the hatchet, Craven, but I have to say it feels refreshing."

"Good, because we can't afford to be fighting with one another any longer. Wellington means to engage Marmont in the North."

"We know. He marched from Rodrigo on the thirteenth."

"Then it has begun. We have not fought a French army inside Spain since Talavera, did you know that?"

"It's about time!"

"What are you doing out here anyway?"

"Mopping up French scouts and messengers wherever we can find them. Wellington wants the enemy to be left in the dark. He would rob them of sight and sound and left in total confusion, but our work is not done yet."

"Then you do not march to join the army?"

"Soon, but there have been reports of French presence a few miles ahead. It is on our path anyway."

"Is this a fight we must have or one you want to have?"

"Is there a difference?" Timmerman laughed as he upped the pace of his horse further.

Craven looked back to Matthys who only shrugged, for Craven knew precisely what he would say. Good can be done even it is for bad reasons. Craven smiled and spurred his horse on after his old nemesis.

"That man may no longer want you dead, Sir, but he could still be the death of you," insisted Paget as he rode up beside Craven.

"Is he doing anything we would not?"

Paget shrugged as he supposed not. They soared on into the next valley where in the distance they could see French cavalrymen looting a line of Spanish carts filled with fruit picked from the fields.

"Are those scouts, Sir?" Paget asked.

"They might as well be. For any French eyes close to our army are a risk."

"Then we should see to it that they cannot go on with their

work!" Paget roared as if he needed to justify it to himself, whilst everyone else needed no convincing, not even Matthys.

The two forces descended on the French cavalry with a thunderous approach, outnumbering the enemy three to one. The French cavalrymen began to panic and rushed for their horses, but momentum was already in the favour of Craven and Timmerman's combined force as they closed the distance rapidly. They were within fifty yards before the first Frenchman was able to get his horse moving to attempt to flee. Moxy brought his own horse to a stop and took aim at the man. He shot him from the saddle with precision whilst the others stormed onwards, firing pistols and carbines with wild abandon and excitement. One French officer drew his sabre and went at Craven, wanting to at least have a fighting chance. He directed a well-aimed thrust at Craven who parried it away with his broad bladed sabre. Both of them came about and closed in to trade blows at close range.

Sparks flew as the two blades clashed. Craven was impressed with the man's skill, but finally, as the man overextended with a cut to Craven's head, he leaned out and let his adversary's blow pass before him. The man went off balance. Craven stood up in his saddle and directed his sabre for the man's neck, yet he paused for a moment as the Frenchman looked up in horror at the great cleaving blade poised to separate his head from his shoulders. He did not even try to resist now as there was no time, but Craven stayed his hand and remained frozen with his blade held aloft.

"Will you surrender?" Craven asked calmly.

"Oui, Oui, I will." He weakened his grip on his sabre so that it dangled from only two fingers at the war iron. He got upright as Craven lowered his sabre, and the French officer called out to his men to stop fighting.

"They've had enough!" Craven roared.

"You would take prisoners?" Birback was amazed at his action.

"Out in the wilderness we often cannot, but now we are within reach of the army we have a duty to do so, and something might be learned from these men."

The ragged men under Timmerman's command looked to their commander for confirmation as if it was an alien concept to them, and they would not accept Craven's order. But Timmerman shrugged them off as he looked to Craven.

"We are not executioners. Victory is ours, and the spoils, too. There need not be any more death."

Several of Timmerman's men groaned in disappointment, but they obliged nonetheless as the Frenchmen put their weapons down. The French officer still held out his sabre for Craven to take.

"Give me your word you will not raise it again and you may keep it."

"Thank you," he replied in surprise, taking it back in hand and sheathing the sword by his side.

"Lieutenant Normant," he declared as he introduced himself.

"Major Craven."

"Ha, then I do not feel so upset in defeat."

"You know me?"

"Out here at the edges of the frontier in Spain I hear your name often, and always for the same reason. Having crossed swords with you and having lived, I can call my days as an officer well lived."

"And yet you lost?" Paget drew up beside them.

"I imagine you have fought your Major many times, no?" Normant asked him.

"Yes, of course."

"And have you ever defeated him?"

Paget was taken aback by the question as it left him deep in thought.

"I may have lost this battle, but I live on with my honour intact, and that is a victory," added Normant.

"You are a fine swordsman. What a pity we must fight on different sides," replied Craven.

"Perhaps one day England and France will be allies?" Paget asked.

Craven instinctively laughed as he thought of the history of the two nations, but the Frenchman remained surprisingly hopeful.

"No war lasts forever, and so perhaps once day we may ride together," he declared with much enthusiasm as if nothing could get him down.

"How can you stay so positive in the face of defeat?" asked Paget in amazement. The young officer seemed to be mirror of himself but with a level of positivity he had long forgotten.

"I love life, and all that life gives me. Today I got to do battle with a great and famous swordsman, and I lived to tell the tale."

"And tomorrow will give you internment as a prisoner of war."

"A new experience," he smiled.

Paget sighed. The man was insufferable, but Craven could

only laugh at his discomfort. It was the same frustration he had once felt upon meeting a young and naïve Ensign Paget.

"Quite the success, wouldn't you say?" Timmerman asked.

Craven nodded in agreement as he looked back to Normant, wondering if he would be willing to help.

"Tell me, Lieutenant, what were you doing in these parts?"

"We were escorting a messenger, but my troop came under attack, and we lost many. With nothing to sustain us we were forced to find whatever we could to feed us," he replied without hesitation.

There were no great secrets revealed, but it did speak volumes about the enemy presence in the area.

"They have no idea, do they, Sir?" Paget asked.

"No idea about what?"

Nobody said a word, but it was too late, as it was obvious to what Paget was referring.

"Wellington is on the move against Marshal Marmont, isn't he?"

Craven did not deny it and that was confirmation enough.

"I wish you every luck, Sir!"

"You wish us luck against your own army?" Paget asked in disbelief.

"You seem like good men, and I would wish good luck to all good men, no matter which uniform they wear or flag which they fight for."

Paget sighed, for he found the Frenchman's enthusiasm stifling.

Craven noticed Birback rifling through the pockets of the dead and suddenly felt shame overcome him.

"Enough," he declared.

"Do not stop on my part, Major. A soldier must do what he must do, and it would be a terrible thing for anything to go to waste which another man might find use or value, but I would ask one simple favour."

"What is it?"

"May we be allowed to bury our fallen? They were good men, all of them."

Craven looked to the others with confusion and finally to Matthys. He was not accustomed to such a circumstance, for they commonly left the French dead where they had killed them. Matthys' expression spoke volumes as Craven suddenly felt a little guilt overcome him.

"Of course, of course."

Normant went to the carts that they had been pillaging for food and had been abandoned by those driving them. He dug out some shovels and threw them to his men whilst going to work with one himself as Craven and his comrades watched. It was a peculiar scene. They had watched their own dead be buried many times and even had to dig many graves themselves, but as the watched the enemy go to work it was hard to not see the similarities and feel the same way they did upon burying their own.

"I shouldn't think any of them deserved to die here today."

Paget was the only one who could find the words many of them were feeling and also be brave enough to say it.

"War is awful business," stated Matthys.

"There is nobility in it, or there can be, but the death is abhorrent, for all but the very worst of our enemies."

It was clear that the scene brought the horrors home to Paget in a way no other sight ever had. He looked upon the grave diggers with more horror than he had witnessed at Rodrigo and Badajoz. Not because the scene was as gruesome, but because it gave a perspective he had never considered.

"Is it futile? War, I mean?"

"It can be, but not this one, not for us," replied Matthys.

"But that man, that Lieutenant, that could just as easily have been me if I were born in France and not England."

"Perhaps."

"He seems like a good fellow, and yet he fights for the enemy, who invade and conquer everywhere they go?"

"I am sure he believes in what he is doing, because he was brought up to do so, just like you were," added Craven.

Paget was stunned as he knew it to be true. He thought back and realised he would have gone on service anywhere and waged war against any enemy he had been ordered to fight against. The realisation had a profound effect on his entire outlook as he thought back to the early days of his encounters with Craven and the others. He looked to Craven and could not remain silent any longer.

"Sir, when we first met, I thought you were lazy, or selfish, without any care for anyone else. I thought you ignored orders because of these reasons, but I was wrong, wasn't I?"

"No, not really."

Paget did not know how to respond.

"I was all of those things. I did not resist orders and my duty because it was the right thing to do. I was not a good man."

"I am not sure I was any better. My morals were based on only what I had told was correct and not what I believed in my heart. I complied and thought it was right and just, but you resisted but not for the right reasons."

"You were always a better man than I ever was," insisted Craven as he could see Paget spirally into self-doubt.

"And look at you now, both men who are ten times better than you ever were upon when first you met," declared Matthys.

"Is that true? Are you sure?" Paget was horrified by the suggestion.

"I know it is."

"How, how can you know?"

"Because a man who had not become a much better version of himself would never ask these questions."

Craven patted Matthys on the shoulder, thankful of the support.

"Then there are good men that we face in battle, and it horrifies me."

"We cannot think about it like that. You cannot, or it will destroy you," replied Matthys.

"How can I not?"

"Because this war is greater than any of us. We do not exist in a perfect world where we make the best decisions for the right reasons. We do the best we can. We cannot change the fact we have to fight men like Lieutenant Normant, but that doesn't mean we cannot show him respect and do all that we can for him when the power is in our hands."

Matthys almost came to tears as he heard Craven speak the words that he himself would have expected to have to explain in years gone by.

They watched as the French soldiers finalised the simple graves they had completed, and they paid their last respects.

Normant returned to them.

"Thank you, you are good men."

Paget began to cry as it was overwhelming, and he tried to hide it.

"Paget, is it?" Normant placed a hand on his heart.

"I thank you, for I too weep, but I also celebrate the men we lost here today, for they lived a good life, an honest life. And I can see that you do, too, or you would never weep for your fallen enemies, but we are enemies no longer. For this war is over for me, and now we are merely soldiers in different uniforms."

"We should be on our way," insisted Timmerman.

"I am sorry, but he is correct," replied Craven.

"No, thank you, Major. Please now lead the way to the next stage in our lives."

They formed up with the prisoners in a column between Timmerman's cavalry leading the way and Craven's bringing up the rear.

"How, but how can he stay so positive, Sir?" Paget asked Craven as they got underway.

"I have often wondered the same about you. I used to find that part of you most annoying, but now I find myself missing it. Don't ever lose that side of you, for it is one of your greatest strengths."

"They are not all bad, are they?"

"The French?"

"Yes, Sir."

"No, they are not, and not all of us are good either."

"I imagined they were. I truly hoped that they were."

"I know," admitted Craven as he remembered how blindly

Paget followed the patriotic rhetoric when he first arrived in the Peninsula.

"I think I finally realise why you were so averse to being a soldier."

"You give me too much credit. I certainly had a reluctance to do my duty, but it was not out of a sense of good and evil but knowing you has made me wish that it was."

"You think knowing me has made you a better soldier, Sir?"

"Certainly, but that is not what I meant. You have driven me to be a better man."

The knowledge put Paget at ease more than Craven had expected as it reminded him of the good in the world and how much of an impact he could have.

"Then I must keep up my work," he replied with a little of the enthusiasm he seemed to have lost.

"See that you do, because we are relying on you."

"You are, Sir?"

"Yes," he replied honestly.

They marched on, and within a few hours they were reaching the edge of Wellington's camp where they handed off their prisoners as quickly as possible.

"Thank you, Major Craven," declared Normant as they parted ways.

"And to you, Lieutenant. When this war is over, you come and find me, you hear?"

"Truly?"

"I have many friends who were once my enemies, and one day I would gladly count you amongst them."

"I look forward to it," beamed Normant before they were

led away.

"Did you mean that, Sir?"

"A man who can fight like that and keep such a strong spirit even in defeat, I wish we could all be a little more like that."

"And yet he has failed his country."

"I'm not sure he sees it rather that way, and neither do I."

Craven's response caused Paget to become lost in his own thoughts as he mulled it over.

"Craven!"

It was Major Spring approaching at speed, but he did not stop and gestured for Craven to follow with him.

"Yes, Sir?"

"Damn good work at Almaraz. It could hardly have gone better, well except for Miravete, that would have been a feather in Hill's cap," replied Spring, referring to the castle to the South of the bridge which they had to abandon the attack on.

"We were told an enemy army was approaching, Sir."

"Yes, according to Erskine." Spring was seething with anger.

"And they were not?"

"There is no evidence to suggest it, no, nor any explanation where that damned fool could have heard it, but no matter, the bridge is gone and onwards we go."

"And so is all to plan?"

"As much as a thing can ever be, yes, but I have some troubling reports," he replied as they approached Wellington's tent. They rushed inside to find him alone and deep in thought. He was studying a map of the area.

"What is it?" Wellington demanded as if he was not lost in the map at all and well aware of their presence.

"The latest reports from our Spanish allies."

Spring tossed a leather satchel violently down on Wellington's map table. The General did not seem bothered by it, as he looked to Craven who was covered in dust and dirt from his several days in the saddle.

"Well, Major, I hear you have been busy."

"Yes, Sir, but I am afraid the enemy now know you are not advancing South."

"How could they know that?" Spring demanded.

"Colonel Mizon, Sir. I met with him under a white flag, and despite no mention on my part, he's discovered our plan."

"No matter now, we are here, and our plans are no secret any longer. We march for Salamanca, though initial reports suggest Marmont is evacuating the city. He will not stand and fight, more's the pity."

"I really think you should read these reports, Sir."

Spring pointed to the satchel on the table between them. Wellington sighed and finally obliged. He opened the documents and took a considered look.

"This estimates Marmont's strength at almost fifty thousand," he fumed before slamming them back down.

"Yes, Sir," replied Spring.

"It cannot be true. He cannot have that many. I do not believe it. Our Spanish friends worry too much and overstate his strength."

"One would hope so, Sir."

"If it is true, then we do not have the advantage in numbers we thought?"

"Indeed, Major, we would be of equal strength, including Spanish troops which have not yet been tested," sighed

Wellington.

"Do you think it to be true, Sir?"

"It cannot be. Why would Marmont flee the city if he had such a strong force?"

Neither of them answered as they did not want to speculate, and it didn't seem like Wellington was really looking for their input, more he wanted to release his own frustrations.

"We keep marching on, and we march until Marmont will face us."

"Sir, he might withdraw his main force from Salamanca, but I do not believe he will abandon it completely," replied Spring.

"Damn it, the French have spent years chasing us and pressing for open battle, and now we offer it to them, and they will not stand and fight?" Wellington asked in frustration.

"They are smart. For we are finally strong enough to scare them, and they know it," replied Craven.

"Yes, that is what worries me."

"What can I do, Sir?"

Wellington sighed as he rested back and thought about it all.

"You have done plenty, Major. Rest easy, and tomorrow you will remain with the army. Marmont plays tricks on us, and I would have a gambling man at hand to counter him."

"I am a bad gambler, Sir."

Wellington and Spring looked at one another and laughed, which was a welcome relief from the tense situation.

"Nice of you to finally admit it, Major," smiled Wellington.

"You might have been a rich man by now if you had been

a less frivolous man," added Spring.

"Yes, but then I wouldn't be me, would I?"

"Quite so, it is not just our successes which define us, but also our defeats and the challenges we face," admitted Wellington.

"Thank you, Sir, will that be all?"

"Yes."

"Oh, Craven?" Spring stopped him from leaving.

"Yes, Sir?"

"Do me a favour."

"Yes, Sir?"

"The next time you see Colonel Mizon, you make sure it is the last, is that understood?"

"Yes, Sir."

He left the tent feeling rage pulse through his hands as they formed fists. He wished he had ended the French Colonel when he had the chance, but he was glad he had not. For the truce which had existed for those moments was sacred to him, but it was no less frustrating, as he knew Mizon would go on to cause them all sorts of trouble whilst he remained alive.

Salamanca it is, then.

Craven wondered where they would next meet the enemy. It was the battle they had all been waiting for, and yet with Marmont withdrawing his main force, it left them all wondering if the great clash would ever come. They had anticipated a great field battle with the enemy since Talavera. The wait seemed to go on forever, and yet the two great armies were so close now a confrontation seemed inevitable.

CHAPTER 9

"Will it finally happen, Sir? Will we finally meet the French army in open battle?" asked Paget excitedly as he returned to the modest camp they had established amongst the vast army they now marched with. They had found as quiet a spot as possible, but there were still thousands of soldiers in sight, many eagerly chatting away about what the coming days and weeks might bring.

"No," he replied bluntly.

Paget sighed with frustration, but it did not surprise him.

"We are too strong for them, and they now run from us like when we ran for Lisbon and the Lines," declared Paget.

"One can hope so."

"You do not believe it, Sir?"

"A clever man fights on the ground of his choosing. I am not so sure the French are running."

That was even more of a concern for Paget who looked

anxious by the prospect.

"I can't take this waiting any longer. It is too much."

Craven grunted in agreement.

"We still march on Salamanca?" Matthys asked.

"We do."

"It may not be the victory we would have wanted, but it will mean the world to the people of that city," insisted Ferreira compassionately, "We know what it is like to have the French take our homes from us in a way I do not think you can truly understand."

"And I hope I never do, but the truth is, Portugal and Spain, they feel as much like home to me as England, as much as I ever truly had a home," replied Craven.

"Salamanca is a beautiful city, and I would very much like to see it again," added Vicenta.

"And you will," insisted Craven.

"Major." Paget gestured over Craven's shoulder, and he turned about to see General Le Marchant approaching.

"Good evening, Sir."

But Le Marchant was far more casual as he approached and put a hand on Craven's shoulder. He smiled at him.

"I see you still have that purse of money I gave you. At least you have not spent it, but I presume that means you come back empty-handed?"

"I do, but I have a sword in mind."

"Do you?" Le Marchant responded with great curiosity.

"A most fine sword indeed, a rival of my own but even more beautiful."

"A sword must look presentable, but you know that I care about its usefulness more than anything."

"It will handle supremely."

"You have handled it, then?"

"Not exactly."

"No, then?"

Craven shrugged.

"I am sorry I am not yet in possession of it," he apologised.

"Oh, no, I toy with you, Major. Duty comes before all else, and you have had plenty of work to keep you busy. And from I hear you did not waste a moment."

"There is no shortage of work to be done when the French are everywhere throughout this land."

"Indeed, and I would hope we could have done some work."

"From what I hear you have been busy, too, Sir, leading a cavalry charge."

"Villagarcia, yes, we were indeed triumphant, but I fear there is little for us to do until Marshal Marmont stops running away."

"He will be drawn into battle soon enough."

"You are sure?"

"I am sure the French will not allow a British army to march across Spain unopposed, yes."

Le Marchant took a deep breath as he looked out across the vast army which was now fading into the night.

"I always dreamt of this, you know? I never truly got to have the glory days in my youth that I would have wanted. Our campaign in the Low Countries is a distant memory and will never be remembered fondly by anyone, but here and now I have my chance once more, before I am too old for it all."

"How old are you, Sir, if you do not mind me asking?"

"I will be forty-seven this summer, a few years older than our Lord Wellington."

"And you think he will stop anytime soon?"

"No," smiled Le Marchant.

"You will outlive us all and command an army of your own, I am sure of it."

"One step at a time. It was a struggle enough to leave England."

"We march on to victory, Sir."

"Of course, we do," Le Marchant smiled again as he perked up.

"Good to see you, Craven." He patted him on the back and wandered on into the night.

Craven looked across the small fire and found Ferreira peering out into the darkness lost in his thoughts. Craven went to him, but the Portuguese Captain spoke as he approached without turning to face him, showing he was not lost at all.

"I wish I'd gone with you."

"No, you don't."

"I'd take facing the enemy over dealing with some of the truly awful so-called gentlemen of this army."

"Blakeney again?"

Ferreira nodded in agreement.

"I should have known."

"Yes, I agree with that sentiment."

"What is it this time?"

"Everything. Anything. Deal with him, or I will."

"You cannot go near him, and you know it."

Ferreira shrugged.

"Perhaps we will get lucky, and he'll be injured in combat and sent home never to return."

"I don't believe we will have such luck. For dogs like him just somehow persist whilst good soldiers die in droves."

"Don't worry about Blakeney. A great battle is upon us and that is all that matters." Although Craven knew it would do little to placate his Portuguese friend, as he was equally as furious, and he had not even had to deal with the awful officer.

"He took our wine and everything else the Lady Sarmento sent for us. A horde the likes of which I have never seen. We would have feasted liked kings."

Craven hissed angrily as he was seething now.

"And you let him?" he snapped.

"I had no choice. For if I was to resist, we would all look like greedy fools."

Craven sighed as he did not know the circumstances, but he trusted Ferreira.

"I met with Mizon whilst we were out there," revealed Craven.

"The French Colonel?" Ferreira sounded surprised at that.

"Indeed."

"Why, oh why would you do that?"

"He offered me riches. And to join the winning side."

Ferreira chuckled.

"You considered it, then?"

"Not for a moment. I will not die a poor man, but I will not fight for the enemy."

"You were not tempted even for a moment?"

Craven shook his head.

"If Mizon has those riches to offer, then I do not need

them gifted to me. I will take them."

"Good."

But the other part of that story weighed heavily on them both until Ferreira finally said it. "The winning side?"

"I'd like to say I am certain of victory, but there are no certainties in war, and we face a great uphill battle."

"And yet here we are, still pushing forward."

"Mizon says Napoleon has amassed an army of one million soldiers."

Ferreira burst out into laughter.

"What?"

"You really believe that? One million? How would he feed and supply an army of that size?"

Craven shrugged.

"Whether it is that vast or not, there are rumblings of something huge. Some say he could be leading the largest army ever seen. It is hard to comprehend such a vast force and what we could do against it."

"I should slap you," declared Ferreira boldly.

Craven could find no words as he was stunned.

"This talk of what might be and how we might face some goliath of a force, but we have fought against all odds, and we have come out on top, more than once. Do not let the melancholy which came over your brother take you, too."

Ferreira bolstered himself for the response, expecting a fist to his face. But Craven smiled, for it was good to have friends to keep him on course. He reached over with one hand which he placed on Ferreira's shoulder.

"Good, keep it up."

He went over to Matthys to find his own counsel, but he

did not need to ask for it, as his old friend and guide was ready for him.

"They have all been through a lot."

Craven agreed.

"They need a victory. For we have all poured sweat and blood into this effort for years now. Finally, we have our chance at breaking out across Spain. They need a victory, and they need to know it was all worth it."

"I know."

"No matter what happens, we have to meet the enemy in battle, and we must also win," replied Matthys.

"I am surprised you are so eager for it, for such a violent confrontation?"

"Because it must be done."

Craven groaned in agreement.

The next day they were on the road with the army once more. Craven's mounted detachment were ahead of the main column but behind the cavalry scouts who pressed on for the city limits.

"Nice to now be at the forefront for once, isn't it?" Ferreira asked.

Craven shrugged, as he'd gladly accept the danger for the first glimpse of their future.

"I would like to be there when our troops enter the city," claimed Paget boldly.

"Yes? Then let us do it."

Craven launched his horse into action and soared forward. Paget was taken aback for a moment, and it took a few seconds for him to realise what was happening before he went galloping on after the Major. It didn't take long for them to reach the scouts at the forefront of the advance. They were already reaching the city limits where many of the locals had gathered and cried out in celebration, clapping to welcome their liberators as they entered the city.

It was clear they were going to receive a hero's welcome as they continued on. Paget was soon caught up in it all. It was a marvellous spectacle as it was indeed overwhelming. They had become so accustomed to being greeting by terrified civilians as French armies descended upon them, but this was a new experience, and they were embraced by the populace as if they were their countrymen.

"Stay focused. We do not know what enemy presence remains."

"Yes, Sir," apologised Paget.

But British, Portuguese, and Spanish troops continued to flood into the city and were in no doubt who was in command of Salamanca. They watched Wellington be escorted by a triumphant force into the Plaza Mayor where the cries of celebrations reached their crescendo. The local men and women pawed at Wellington, and many hugged him, interrupting him at every stage as he tried to write down and pass on new orders.

Yet Craven ignored it all and continued on through the streets, and it was not long until they got their first glimpse of the remaining French presence. They could not see a single Frenchman, but the structures they had built to withstand an attack were most formidable. Three convents which were built on high ground at the Southwestern corner of the city had been heavily fortified. Craven studied it carefully for a few minutes when he turned to address Paget and his comrades. Instead, he found Wellington himself in their place where he had escaped the crowds that were now held back in the streets before them. There was a look of stern discomfort on the General's face and that was cause for concern.

"Is everything okay, Sir?" Craven asked.

"No, I was told Salamanca was protected by these three convents, but not that they were so formidable."

Craven nodded in agreement. He had never seen such formidable improvised defensive works. The university and college buildings, as well as many other structures had been knocked down and used to double the walls of the old medieval convents. Oak beams and earth were piled high, all windows had been blocked up, and the approaches to all three fortified with scarps, counterscarps, and palisades. Cannon barrels bristled out from the few openings they could see. The old medieval city walls protected the largest of the convents on two sides, and French cannons covered the Roman bridge to the South.

"They have made a fortress of it," lamented Wellington.

It was remarkable what had been achieved, and it was clearly a very clever and tactical mind who had overseen the works. But to the British troops looking on, it was yet another reminder of the deadly sieges of Rodrigo and Badajoz, and it was as though they could never escape those murderous events.

"It can be overcome."

"We have only a few guns and little ammunition. I was promised these fortifications were of little consequence and nothing to concern myself about."

Craven said nothing as he studied them closely. There would be no easy approach against the forts, except from the North through the city ruins. The enemy knew this, too and had put a great deal of effort into establishing their defences. The roofs of the convents supported field guns, and that could only mean one thing. The enemy had casemated the upper stories of the convents, making them into such strong fortifications that they may support artillery across their roofs, completing a very thorough defensive structure.

"I know it can be overcome, and the whole army knows it. We did not come this far to have our dreams shattered by a few hastily build forts. And how ever many Frenchmen await us, they cannot have more than a thousand between the three of them, and probably less."

Wellington took a deep breath and let the disappointment fade away. He took a leaf from Craven's book and decided to look rather more favourably upon it than his chief engineer.

"Major James Craven, meet Lieutenant Colonel John Fox Burgoyne."

"Taken over from Fletcher, have you?" Craven asked, remembering the wounds the engineer had suffered during Badajoz. He had gotten on well with the man.

Craven remembered this man from Badajoz but had little time to get an impression of him. He was still fresh faced and had surely not yet reached thirty, but he also looked wise beyond his years.

"I believe we have crossed paths many times, but only in passing," replied Burgoyne.

"What do you make of this?" Craven gestured towards the enemy strongholds.

"Worse than anticipated, a lot worse. There is much work to be done, and not near enough guns to batter the enemy like they will need battering."

Burgoyne gave a judgemental look towards Wellington as

if blaming him for that fact.

"Well, what do you suggest?" Wellington asked abruptly.

"We must get our guns in place as quickly as we can. Emplacements must be dug, and if we can use the elevations around us, then we should do so at the earliest."

"Any chance of an assault without bombardment?"

Burgoyne sighed as he didn't seem confident of it.

"Let me go in under cover of darkness and see for myself. If there is a way it can be done, I will find it," declared Craven.

Wellington was taken aback.

"Why would you volunteer for this?"

"Because it's an awful job, and I wouldn't suggest it only to have some other poor bastard have to do it for me."

"Very well, I will leave it to you gentlemen."

"Sir?" Craven asked.

"What is it?"

"Do we attack these forts to take them or to provoke Marmont into launching an attack?"

Wellington only smiled before leaving them be.

"What do you think?" Craven asked Burgoyne.

"I think Lord Wellington hopes for one outcome whilst planning for two."

"And if neither is accomplished. If Marmont is not drawn in and you can't breach those walls?"

"They will be breached. It is only a matter of time."

"And the longer this goes on the more likely Marmont is to be drawn in?"

Burgoyne did not agree to it, but they were both thinking it.

"Time may be on our side, but it will be paid for in lives."

"Is that why you volunteered to go out there tonight?"

Craven shrugged as it was in part true.

They waited and watched for the sun to go down as the work parties assembled with picks and shovels to begin their work establishing emplacements for the cannons so that the bombardment could begin. And yet even in darkness, the French did not give them an easy night. Cannon and musket fire rained down on the work parties.

Craven watched from afar with a few of his closest and most trusted friends as those digging jumped for cover and struggled to make any progress. Many of them were Portuguese and cried out in their own tongue as they leapt to the ground for cover as cannon balls landed around them. Progress was slow and it was a miserable job. The enemy kept on firing without any reason to stop, for nothing was coming back their way. Moxy looked most anxious as he watched the silhouettes of the French soldiers take aim with each shot from the walls, knowing he was quite capable of striking them down when they made their attempts.

"They need sharpshooters knocking them down," insisted Moxy.

"They do, but there is nothing we can do, not now, not unless you want to rain down fire upon us."

Only Paget, Moxy, Ellis, and Vicenta were with him so that they kept as quiet as possible. They watched and waited until the sky was as dark as they could hope for until finally the time had come.

"Everyone ready?" Craven asked.

No words needed to be shared.

"Here, Sir." Moxy handed him one of the last two

Girardoni Air Rifles, the only firearm which could be fired and not draw the attention of the entire garrison to them. Moxy clung onto the other, "Air seals aren't long for this world, but you should get two or three out of her."

It was the huge weakness of the technological marvel that they were. The rifle was certainly a technical marvel and infinitely superior to any musket or rifle at short range, so long as it was in good order, but the propulsion relied entirely on the reservoir of pressurized air. Once the seals holding in that air were compromised the rifle was rendered useless, a detrimental flaw which had kept them from widespread use. Craven had not even brought his own rifle so as to not risk any noise, and so being empty-handed he gladly accepted it. Ellis looked on the exchange with envy.

"Follow me." Craven led them on.

"You trust him with that rifle?" Ellis asked Moxy.

"He is leading the way and most likely to get into trouble. Fair that he gets it, or would you rather lead us?"

Ellis shrugged as he had given up any notion of command a long time ago, and he knew Moxy was playing on that knowledge and mocking him for it. Ellis grumbled at the prospect before following on. The convents were lit up periodically as cannons and muskets ignited, but the approach to them remained in relative darkness. But considering the French garrison was able to see and hear the work details dig the gun emplacements, they knew they had to be careful. Craven darted back and forth amongst the ruins. Where the enemy had demolished so many buildings for materials to build their fortifications, they had left much behind, including many walls intact with which to take cover.

On they crept, as a waft of powder smoke passed them by. It was a tense advance. They knew if they were spotted, they would attract a barrage of fire. The enemy would keenly be looking for anyone attempting to undermine their defences in any way. They covered the first few hundred yards with ease, but as they drew closer, their chances of being found out increased significantly. Particularly as each French cannon erupted as the fifty-foot burst of flames from the muzzle lit up the ground before the fortifications. Craven kept on moving at a cautious but steady pace until he heard voices and dropped down to listen. French voices were communicating with one another not far away. He leant out from the cover of a wall and could see the French pickets deep in conversation, but he was equally surprised as he turned back to see a dozen British soldiers approaching them.

"What are you doing?"

"Providing some assistance," declared the Lieutenant leading the party.

Craven sighed as he appreciated the sentiment but knew they would only increase their chances of being discovered by the enemy, but he could not send them away now as they had shown great bravery in coming out to support him.

"That is quite the weapon you have there, Sir." The Lieutenant was marvelling at the Girardoni Air Rifle, which few in the British army knew existed, let alone had ever laid eyes on one.

"An air weapon, it is near silent."

"Most useful," replied the Lieutenant.

"Come on." He led them far and wide of the French pickets as he periodically stopped and studied the defences.

They were strong in every place he looked, which was disheartening, but he was not about to give up. He stopped once more and peered around a corner to again study the enemy positions, but just a few seconds later he heard a rumbling and angry growl ahead. He looked into the rubble beyond and could see a scruffy salivating dog glaring at them.

"Shit," whispered Craven.

"Use the rifle, Sir. Shoot the dog," insisted the Lieutenant as he thought on his feet and remembered what Craven had told him about the marvellous rifle. The dog growled a little louder, and that was his prompt to bring the rifle to the ready. He cocked back the hammer which made it ready to fire and took aim, causing the dog to bare its teeth further.

"Shoot it, Sir."

But Craven looked back to Paget who was horrified.

"Do it, Sir!" insisted the Lieutenant.

"I can't."

"Give it to me, then."

The Lieutenant tried to take the weapon from Craven, but he shoved the man away, sending him crashing to the ground. The dog growled a little louder until finally erupting into a violent bark.

Craven dropped back down into cover as they all remained still and out of sight, waiting to hear if anything would come of it. The dog continued to bark and soon enough they could hear the cries of the French pickets as they drew closer to investigate.

"Shit," muttered Craven.

The barking continued, and they knew it was only a matter of time before they were discovered.

"Run," ordered Craven sternly, but for a moment nobody moved.

"Run!" he cried out as he got to his feet and sprinted back towards their own lines.

The cries of the French pickets echoed out at their backs as the first few shots rang out. Craven looked back to see the Lieutenant he had shoved away was returning fire with his pistol but was hit by a musket ball in the shoulder just seconds later. Craven rushed back for him and hauled him on as he winced with pain. He tried to turn back to retrieve the pistol he had lost, but Craven pulled him on.

"Leave it! It's not worth your life!"

Musket and cannon fire smashed into the ruins all around them as they darted back and forth between the remaining walls. A musket ball sliced into Craven's hand and another skimmed Moxy's arm, but they ran on. Several more of their party were struck but everyone stayed on their feet and kept running. The relentless fire of musket and cannon did not let up until finally, they reached the cover of the streets of the city which had not been demolished and hurtled themselves into shelter as they gasped for air.

"Everyone still with us?" Craven asked.

"All accounted for," replied Matthys as he went to see about the wounded, despite having a bloody face of his own where shards of stone had cut into his flesh.

"Why, oh, why could you not shoot the damned dog?" demanded the Lieutenant as he winced in pain.

Craven looked to Paget and had his answer.

"Because there has been enough killing, and that animal never did anything to us to deserve death."

"It was working for the enemy!" cried the officer as Matthys checked his wound.

"It was a stray dog and we startled it. The French probably gave that animal food. What did you ever do for it?" Craven snapped back at him.

The Lieutenant groaned but said nothing more.

"Well, that was fruitless," declared Paget.

"Not exactly, we have ruled that out," smiled Craven.

Paget was stunned but finally began to laugh at Craven's dry humour, and the others soon joined them, even though the wounded Lieutenant could not see the funny side of it. He remained stone cold and brooding, which only made Craven laugh more.

CHAPTER 10

First light was upon the city of Salamanca, and it was soon apparent that the work to dig and built the gun emplacements in order to bombard the heavily fortified convents had progressed little. In fact, the trenches were only knee high, and so the men working in them were soon ordered to withdraw, not having cover from the enemy with which to keep up their work. There was nothing to be done in the broad daylight and so the British and Portuguese troops watched the forts from afar, many huddling in the shade of the houses and remaining college buildings. It was a frustrating pause in the campaign. The army had expected to march to face an entire French army and settle it once and for all, but now they were delayed by this great obstacle.

"It is quite the feat, isn't it, Sir?" Paget asked.

"What?"

"To have built such a significant defence in such short a

space of time."

Craven shook his head.

"This was not done in a few days or weeks. Perhaps it was accelerated in that time, but that is the result of months or years of work."

"I thought the enemy were confident in finishing us in Portugal, Sir?"

"Yes, but a wise man prepares for all eventualities, and Salamanca is of great importance to Napoleon. It is an important city, a through road, and a symbol of French power in this region. To conquer it would mean only a short hop on to Madrid."

"But for how ever strong it is, it cannot withstand us, can it?"

Craven shrugged.

"Then the enemy mean to hold us here long enough to gather their strength?"

"Yes, and they will come at us. The only question is when."

"I am sick of the waiting."

"But Wellington is not."

"How so, Sir?"

"Because he fights where he wants and when, a great defender," replied Ferreira wearily as if Paget should know.

"Is that right, Sir?" Paget asked Craven.

But he did not answer, and Paget knew it to be true as he had experienced it himself on many occasions.

"Will Marshal Marmont come, Sir?"

"Oh, he will indeed."

"But when, Sir, when?"

"If you want insight into the mind of a French General, then you are asking the wrong man," sighed Craven.

They watched as hundreds of riflemen of the King's German Legion marched into the area. They began to spread out amongst the ruins where they had crept through the night before.

"Finally," declared Moxy, glad that sharpshooters had at last come to give support. The riflemen spread out and soon began to give harassing fire. Each man targeted any small opening that presented itself and began to take their toll on the enemy and make their life difficult.

"You can go and join them if you like," Craven offered to Moxy.

"They are doing just fine. I will save my strength for whatever ridiculous plan you have in store next."

"You think me a fool to look for some way to end this sooner?"

"No, I just wish it didn't involve us almost being slaughtered doing so," smiled Moxy.

"You're still here, aren't you?"

"Just about."

Moxy groaned and looked around at their bedraggled state. Most of those who had gone with him the night before were now bandaged up or showing light wounds. They could hear the sound of angry exertions and noticed dozens of soldiers struggling to move two guns up and into the upper floor of a convent to the Northwest of the enemy positions. Loud grunts and groans and a great deal of blasphemy echoed out as they struggled with ropes to hoist the guns up into the elevated positions.

The work went on, and finally, the guns opened fire as those in the British occupied convent duelled with the cannons in the French occupied convents. It was an exhausting thing to watch, and little progress was made as the day went on. Craven and his comrades merely sat in the shade all day, sipping at their drinks and watching the siege go on at a slow pace. It was indeed a slow grind as skirmishers exchanged fire and the cannons roared all day, but the one thing the attackers were certain of, the French had no means of resupply. They could not replace a single soldier lost, and every wounded man only added to their woes. Every cannon ball fired, and all powder expended, dwindled their resources further. For now, the besiegers simply had to keep up the pressure, and it seemed success would follow. Yet a steady stream of wounded hobbled or were carried away to the surgeons. Most were gunners who were under concentrated enemy fire from every loophole as the day went on and they tried to man the guns the best they could.

Paget looked most uncomfortable by the scenes until he finally boiled over.

"Will you do nothing whilst these fine men are killed and wounded?"

"Nothing? Did we do nothing at Almaraz? What about when we worked alongside De Rosas?" Craven replied calmly.

"But those days are already gone."

"And what do you think those gunners were doing whilst we were out fighting?" Matthys jumped to Craven's defence.

"I do not know."

"A soldier cannot be fighting every day. You have lived a whirlwind life since joining us, Mr Paget, and I think you must assume that soldiering is always like it is for you and us, but it is not."

"No?"

Craven shook his head.

"Soldiering is mostly boring," admitted Craven.

"I fear you have come to expect too much of us," added Matthys.

Paget only looked more anxious. He was eager to do something as he shot up and paced back and forth.

"The energy you find is miraculous, but you have done enough, at least for now. Our time will come again," insisted Craven.

But Paget was not comfortable with lying idle, even if it was for a few days, and yet Charlie smiled. She watched him with her feet up on one chair as she sat on another, sipping on her wine as if it were some sort of holiday.

"I thought we were marching to the great battle of our time, Sir. The battle we were all promised. I had prepared myself for it, and now we are stuck with this."

They were all anxious for the battle, it was true, but most were glad of a moment's rest before the time came to fight Marmont's army. Paget sighed as he finally sat back down, knowing he would not get a rise from any of them who were glad of a little time to recuperate. They slept that night in the ruins of the old stone building they has used for shelter from the sun. The next day was much the same, and Craven soon fell asleep in his chair, but early in the afternoon they heard the cry of messengers.

"What is it?" Paget asked of a passing orderly.

"Marmont is on the move. He has driven our cavalry back and approaches from the North!" cried the man with excitement as he rushed on, "Marmont is coming! To arms!" he roared with much enthusiasm.

Paget hurried to gather up his things as Craven awoke and heard the news. It was still being shouted by the same man who had delivered the news to Paget.

"It is happening, Sir!" Paget fixed the clasp of his sword belt and was now fully ready to march or fight. Yet he waited for Craven's orders, not knowing what to expect.

"There is nothing for us to do here. Let us ride North and see this for ourselves."

"Huzzah!" Paget cried.

Though none of the others were quite so eager. For many of them it was a battle they had hoped would never need to be fought. Some amongst the army hoped the French would withdraw to France once the pressure was upon them, but there was no such luck, as whispers and discussion echoed out all around from the troops in the city. Some were already moving to join Wellington in the North, but for many they had to stay to keep the garrison of the three fortified convents contained. Else they would break out and undo all the work that had already been done and spike the guns that had been put in place, or worse, carry them away with them. Those staying behind watched them leave with great anticipation and also concern. For it was a terrible thing to not know what was unfolding when so much was at stake.

They collected their horses from a ruined house being used as their stable and galloped on through the city until they were on their way north and climbing the San Cristobal heights where Wellington had formed up defensive lines in anticipation of an assault by Marmont.

San Cristobal was an elevated position four miles North of Salamanca, which would provide the perfect location to withstand Marmont. It was a typical Wellington strategy in every way as he enticed the enemy to attack the slopes he guarded. Craven raced on towards the scene where he could see infantry forming up on the slopes ahead, but it was the cavalry reserve he encountered first. He came to a halt as he approached Le Marchant, noting the three thousand Spanish infantry also held in reserve, but for very different reasons.

"Is it the day, Sir?"

Paget smiled, realising Craven was as eager as he was to face the French army. He was just better at hiding it. Many of the heavy cavalry troopers looked down upon those riding with Craven. They did not much appreciate his red-coated infantrymen being mounted as if they were imposters, for the heavy cavalry also wore red tunics unlike the British light cavalry in their beloved blue.

"Only two men can know that, and they have to be in agreement!" Le Marchant laughed, referring to Wellington and Marmont. Both would have to commit their forces to an all-out field battle if it was to be settled.

Craven looked over to the heavy cavalry behind Le Marchant, all carrying their huge straight swords with broad dish-hilts. It was a formidable sword indeed, but Craven would never want to give up such dexterity. He noticed Le Marchant did not either. He still he wore the Light Cavalry Sabre he had helped pioneer and adored so much. By regulation he should not have it, but who was going to tell him so?

"I fear the battle might be decided up there without us," said Le Marchant, knowing his cavalry would have little to do if

Marmont's columns were broken on the advance towards the heights.

"There will be no shortage of work to be done, I am sure of it," insisted Craven.

"We can only hope."

Craven peered over the General's shoulder to see the disapproving looks he was receiving from a number of the officers.

"Don't mind them," insisted Gaspard.

"I don't. Men have looked at me like that my whole life, and most of them came to regret it," smiled Craven.

"Now, now, Major, there are enough enemies for us to fight in front of us. Let us not fight those behind us also."

"Yes, Sir."

"Good luck, Major."

Craven led his party on, making their way up to the heights. The army was already formed in their battle lines, ready for anything. He gestured for his party to hold back as he advanced Wellington and his staff who looked down to the open ground below where the French now advanced. Wellington heard his horse approach and smiled at the sight of him.

"Come to see for yourself, have you, Craven!"

"I have, Sir," he admitted.

He looked down to see three vast French columns making their approach. There seemed no sign of them stopping, as if they were going to march straight up the slopes in a direct assault.

"Will they do it, Sir. Will they come?"

"We can only hope."

The enemy continued to advance, tens of thousands of

enemy soldiers progressed towards them up the gentle climbs of the sparse landscape, but as they came within one thousand yards most came to a halt, and the closest unit stopped eight hundred yards short of the British and Portuguese lines. Craven smiled as he thought how disappointed Moxy would be. For he could not make such a shot, but he knew the Welshman would be eager to point out the advantage gained in firing down at a target and the benefit in range it might give. The lines came to a complete standstill, but soon enough the cannons on both sides opened fire, beginning a duel that went on throughout the day, and yet wait and wait they did. Soon the sun was going down, and with it the chances of an engagement that day. However, as they went into the evening, they heard musket fire far into the distance. They raised their spyglasses but could see nothing.

"They make a push on Morisco," declared Wellington as if he knew the area well, which he did because he had spent endless hours poring over maps and spoke of the area as if were his homeland.

Craven took out his map and could see the tiny village to the Northeast of Salamanca.

"Then Marmont means to make an attack?"

"It would seem so. The army will remain in their battle lines this night," ordered Wellington.

"What can I do, Sir?"

"Get what sleep you can and be ready for a fight in the morning."

"Yes, Sir."

He rode back to his comrades who had found a patch of ground to rest out the night, for they were not included in the order of battle and would go where they were needed. The ground around them was barren without even firewood, though the Spanish locals soon began to deliver wood and food to them as best as they could. The thought was appreciated, but they could hardly cater for the more than forty thousand soldiers spending the night on the hillside.

"What news?" Ferreira asked.

"The enemy attack a village called Morisco."

Amyn smirked at the name in a rather uncharacteristic fashion.

"What is it?" Craven asked him.

"That name."

"Moriscos are Moors who were ordered to convert by the church in Spain. It must have been home to such people a long time ago," explained Ferreira.

"Yes, until they were expelled more than two hundred years ago," added Amyn.

Paget was both intrigued and saddened by the story, and even Craven felt for their foreign friend. He had no understanding of the history of it all, but he knew Amyn had entirely lost one home already, and this was a bitter reminder of it.

"Tomorrow the enemy will come, then?" Ferreira asked.

"That is the hope," sighed Craven.

The whole army spent the night in place on the exposed heights. They could not risk being caught by surprise out of order at first light. Yet first light came, and the battle lines redressed and brought to the ready, but there was no sign of the enemy. Craven again went forward but this time with Paget in tow. They returned to Wellington's side as he and his staff watched anxiously for Marmont to make a move. In the distance they could see many more thousands of French troops approaching to bolster their numbers, and Wellington shook his head in disbelief.

"It is true, then, the report of their number?"

"So it would seem, Major. Still, damn tempting! I have a great mind to attack 'em."

But Paget shook his head as he looked back to Craven, knowing their leader would never risk it.

"You don't think he means it?" Craven whispered.

"Of course not. Sir Arthur waits for the enemy to come for us and fight with all the advantages which we have," replied Paget confidently.

But the army waited anxiously for news as the cannons of both sides still duelled throughout the day, but there was no movement. Major Thornhill approached the two officers, glad of less stuffy company than Wellington's staff.

"Funny business, isn't it? Two armies ready to fight and neither willing to take the first step."

"What of Morisco?" Craven asked.

"Wellington ordered our boys back from there in the night, but they made quite an account of themselves, having never seen any action before now."

It was one of the rare occasions he had praised anyone, and that got Craven's attention.

"What now, Sir?" Paget asked.

"Now we wait and hope Marmont draws impatient. He played for time so that he might gather his strength, but now he has it he must decide if he is to attack."

"And will he, Sir? Will he?"

"Who can say, but I imagine the enemy will have a great

deal to discuss this night."

The day passed with no major movements, but the tension remained like a thick cloud of powder smoke hanging over them as they remained in place. The local populace once more brought food, water, and firewood for the army, celebrating them as heroes even though they had not yet accomplished a victory. The Salfords built what modest fires they could, burning anything they could find, including brush as fuel was sparse.

"Will the enemy come tomorrow, Sir?"

Craven shrugged as he had no idea what would happen.

"Evening, gentleman!" Timmerman came to join them.

"Evening, Sir," replied Paget in a friendly fashion, "We were just postulating on whether battle will be upon us tomorrow, whether either army will make a general advance."

"I shouldn't think so," he replied confidently.

"No?"

"Wellington underestimated the enemy strength and is now fearful of risking his entire army at once. And the French, well they look up at a strong force commanded by a very competent defensive General and are reminded of Bussaco and Fuentes. They have been stung before in these very circumstances, and so now they do not want to make the same mistake again."

Craven was stunned by his informed and considered assessment.

"Then we are at a stalemate?"

"For now, but it will not last. Neither army can stay in the field forever, and both need a victory as much as the other," replied Craven.

"And when that battle comes, will you stand with us?"

Paget asked Timmerman as if testing his devotion to his newly found friends.

"I wouldn't miss it for the world," he declared boldly.

The morning soon came after an uneasy night on the heights once again. Still the French did not advance in the morning as the two armies gazed upon one another just outside of musket and rifle range. But the British and Portuguese watched as Wellington sent a division towards Morisco to take the village back.

"Is this it, Sir?" Paget asked.

"Only if Marmont takes the bait," replied Craven.

For he knew that is what the advance was. Wellington poking and prodding at Marmont in an attempt to encourage him to make an all-out attack. But to all of their disappointment, the French skirmish lines began to fall back as they prepared to defend Morisco and abandon any effort to take the heights of San Cristobal. Another night passed, and in the morning the French army was nowhere to be seen, having withdrawn far from sight. The chance to force a major confrontation was over, which was a relief in the short-term, but left so many questions in all of their minds. They knew the battle was coming, and the anticipation was a heavy weight on all their shoulders, not just for the risk of death and disfigurement for every soldier, but because it could decide the war in Spain.

CHAPTER 11

The artillery roared as they tried to batter their way into the forts at Salamanca once again. Craven and the Salfords found themselves as an audience to the display once again, since the action to the North at San Cristobal had amounted to nothing. Now all efforts had been put back into overcoming the strong French defensive positions. But something had changed, and it was clear to see. The guns battered the smaller fort of San Cayetano to the East of San Vincente, the largest of the three which was now left alone.

"The guns, Sir, why the change?" Paget asked.

"San Vincente is strong, and we have few guns and little ammunition. I imagine an attempt will be made to seize the lesser fort and then use it as staging post from which to continue the battering once we have the rounds to do so."

"Quite right," declared Wellington.

Paget shot up from his chair in shock at the realisation the

General was amongst them. He was in the street outside the ruined house from where they were watching the bombardment.

"We should have brought guns up from Rodrigo to batter these walls, and a great deal of shot with which to do so," added Wellington.

"Can we not send for them, Sir?"

"It is already being conducted, but time is not on our side. Every day Marmont tries to get around us and he gains in strength. I would press him for battle, but I cannot do that while these obstacles remain in our way. They must be overcome with all haste."

Another volley rang out from the cannons bombarding the San Cayetano fort. The palisade before it had been breached and the parapet damaged also. Yet the guns were now silent, and no attempt was made to reload them.

"Is that it, Sir? Is that all we have?"

"It is."

"But you will order an assault anyway," added Craven cynically.

"I must, for every day we lose here takes us a step further from victory. An assault will cost many lives, but a great many more will be lost if we cannot push on quickly."

"And us, Sir, what are your orders?"

"Marmont has retreated East about five miles, but he flanks the Tormes river and makes continuous threats to cross it and encircle Salamanca. I have sent our cavalry to ensure that does not happen, and I would have you join them at first light. Marmont probes for any weakness. Do not let him find any."

"Yes, Sir."

Wellington left and Craven still had not gotten up from

his chair.

"This is all so exhausting, Sir. Why will Marmont not face us?" Paget demanded.

"Because he is not a fool. Wellington attempts to draw the enemy into a battle they cannot win, and everyone knows it."

Paget sighed with frustration.

"All the years we have been here has been building to this moment, and yet it will not come," he growled.

"Battle will come soon enough. Let us focus on still breathing when it does."

"That should not be difficult, for what is there for us to do?"

But as the day passed into the evening, and more British light infantry began to amass around them, they knew something was afoot. It was a storm. It had to be, but nobody spoke of it so as to not give away any information to the enemy. The sun was going down, and the time for a storm was fast approaching. Everyone knew it as British soldiers gathered about the ruins ready to go forward. Craven crept up to a better position where he could watch it unfold, whilst being fully armed and ready as if he intended to join them.

"Do we storm this evening, Sir?"

"Not us, but these other boys, certainly."

It was ten o'clock and cries rang out as a general advance was called. Four hundred Light infantry stormed forward with ladders in hand. This would not be the storming of an open breach, but an escalade of the walls. It was a far from ideal situation. They did not have the guns to batter down the thick walls, but the soldiers made their advance, nonetheless. A General led them on from the front as he tried to rally their morale. Cannon and musket fire erupted, causing the entire view to be lit as if it were almost day. The storming party rushed on towards the smaller fort whilst under fire from those inside and also the large San Vincente fort. The initial salvo was devastating, with a great many dropping dead or wounded, and yet they still went on. The General patched up a wound he suffered in the opening shot with a handkerchief before going on to lead them forward once more.

"They will never make it, not with all the fire from that fort," wept Paget.

"Come on!" Craven shouted.

He led the riflemen of the Salfords forward into the ruins to join the other sharpshooters who were doing their best to hit any target they could see or at least stop the enemy from having an easy time of it. They took aim and fired their first shots at any small opening they could find, as the defending French troops kept up a thunderous fire. Moxy and several others found their mark, but it made little difference as they looked to the walls of the San Cayetano fort. Two ladders had been placed against it, two of the twenty that had been carried forward, and not a single soldier had managed to start the climb. The General leading them was at the foot of the ladders crying for the soldiers to go on, but he was shot down for the second and last time. The assaulters had lost both their momentum and will to fight, as their officers ordered a withdrawal to save them from a humiliating break, but it was too late as many ran for their lives. The assault was over, and they all knew it as a third of those soldiers who had conducted the venture were now dead or wounded.

"What do we do, Sir?" Paget cried in horror.

"Cover their retreat. It's all to be done!"

Craven hurried to reload his rifle. The sharpshooters amongst the ruins kept up their fire as best they could. Finally, the French volleys stopped, not out of mercy, but most likely to save their powder. They knew they had been victorious and inflicted a horrid defeat, as they cried out in their triumph and further added salt to the wound. And yet sporadic fire continued. A corporal was shot through the body as he past Craven who jumped out from cover and caught the wounded man before he hit the ground.

"Fall back!" Craven hauled the man back to safety, handing him over to his comrades to continue on to the surgeons.

"That could not have gone any worse." Paget looked back at the ground leading to the fortified convent. It was littered with British dead and the ladders that had been left where they fell. French soldiers were already at the walls taking down those two which had been placed against their fortification, likely to be taken away to be used as firewood.

"There will be no taking of these places until they are thoroughly battered," admitted Craven.

"And so it was for nothing? All of those lives lost for nothing?"

"We never know if a thing can be achieved until we try, and there is no shame in trying," replied Matthys.

"What now, Sir?"

"We wait, or the gunners wait for their heavy guns and shot, but we have other work to do. Our kind of work."

They watched as the dead and wounded were recovered. It was a grim job, but at least the enemy let them do it, though not really for mercy's sake, but so that the dead were not left to decay where other men still had to fight.

"Tomorrow, we ride East," declared Craven.

"Why, Sir, does Marmont keep probing across the Tormes when he does not mean to attack?"

"Oh, he means to attack, for certain, but he is trying everything he can to draw us out into a more favourable position. He feints this way and that, looking for his opening. This is merely a duel on a grand scale."

"I wish the games would come to an end, for I would very much like to know the result."

"So would we all, but do not worry, a battle is coming, once both army Commanders agree upon satisfactory terms."

"Not everything is like a duel, Sir," protested Paget.

"Everything? No, but any battle certainly is. Both sides wanted victory and to keep their honour. Both willing to die but praying they do not. They are often fought over trivial matters, but sometimes over the most important of ones. Both believe God is on their side, whilst deep down knowing it is really all about the simplest of things. One's skill, weapon, and a little bit of luck. Some men go on to it drunk and foolish, and others sober but with murderous intent."

Once again, they slept in the ruins of the South edge of Salamanca that night, but it was eerily quiet. There were no gun emplacements to dig and build, and there was no more shot to expend. The enemy did not waste their stores either, as pickets walked quietly about on both sides, knowing it would be a blissful night. The British advance had proven two things. Firstly, the French forts could not be taken without dealing with the most powerful one first, San Vincente. For a frightful fire was maintained from it over the rest of the enemy positions. Secondly, San Vincente would not be taken without a heavy battery from the big guns.

Ferreira awoke restlessly in the night and got up to stretch his legs as he could not sleep. He noticed Paget was awake, too, and leaning against the remains of a wall outside, gazing upon the enemy positions. So he went to join the Lieutenant.

"You cannot sleep either?"

"I wonder how Marmont can be overcome, Sir, how he can be forced into battle."

Ferreira was stunned. He had assumed the young officer was fixated and lamenting the bloody and fruitless assault they had witnessed earlier that day.

"You worry about the problems of a general, when you are not a general," replied Ferreira, thinking it might soothe his mind.

"But I will be, and I would know everything there is to know before that day comes," replied Paget confidently.

Ferreira did not even question it as it would surprise no one if he should rise to such heights.

"Wellington was not born with the knowledge and capability he exhibits today. It was learnt. I wager he spends endless hours considering the moves of those around him, both his own commanders and the enemy."

"I am certain of it, for he has been a soldier for well over twenty years."

"Then I, too, must learn to see these things. I must learn to predict my enemies and learn how to be several steps ahead of them, just like him."

"You make it out to be easy, but it is not. Not even

Wellington has been able to draw Marmont into battle."

"It is only a matter of time. Wellington and Marmont are like two hunters, treating the other like prey, and neither man is willing to go home hungry."

"Yes."

"How can you be so calm, Sir?"

"I suppose because I know that in time, we will be victorious. The people of Spain, just like my people, are entirely hostile to the French. No army can maintain its grip on a people who despise and hate them with a passion like they do. For the people here are nothing if not passionate. We will not grow to accept the French, not in Portugal or Spain. The day an army crossed over the French border to come South was the day France sealed its fate, and I will be there to see it."

"But the army, Sir, the vast army they say Napoleon has created?"

"What of it?"

"It does not concern you, Sir?"

"If it were marching South to face us, yes it would."

"But it is not?"

"No, and so Napoleon now makes his error. He has either decided that those forces he has left here are enough to defeat us, or that Spain and Portugal no longer matter, and he will come to regret it."

"If we can win."

"How can we not? You have seen what this war has done, what men it has made of us. Before it all I did my utmost to never take any risks. Craven was nothing more than a bad gambler with a quick sword hand, and you were a boy still lost in your dreams, but now look at us. What hope is there for the enemy when we have been forged into the soldiers we are today?"

"Boyish dreams, you must think me silly for thinking one day I could lead an army?" Paget replied sheepishly.

"No, that is not a boyish dream, for you are no longer a boy. That is the ambition of a man who knows he will achieve it, and you will."

"I will, Sir?" Paget replied in disbelief.

"Yes, you will, and when that day comes, I will proudly follow you."

Paget was close to tears.

"I thought the prospect of promotion to such heights was dead once I had chosen to remain with Craven."

"For him, it surely is, and he would not have it any other way, but you can go on to heights the rest of us can only dream of."

Paget took a deep breath and felt a great deal of weight lifted as he imagined his future was finally in good hands.

"Come on, let's get some rest," insisted Ferreira.

And yet they noticed Birback, Moxy, Ellis, and Vicenta creeping off with Timmerman and several of his men.

"Should we say something, Sir?"

"Whatever trouble they are looking for is their own."

Paget grumbled and went on to find his makeshift bed, but he noticed Craven was missing, too. He grumbled a little more before attempting to heed Ferreira's advice, but he could not settle and shot back up to chase on after Timmerman and the others. He followed them to the quiet parts beyond the city and tried to creep up cautiously, only to find a knife at his throat in the darkness. He gasped in horror.

"Mr Paget?" Vicenta asked, who retracted her blade.

"What is the meaning of this?" he demanded angrily.

Though in truth he was glad the dark night hid his pale face and look of terror.

"Look." Craven appeared before them and pointed out to the grape vines all about the hills around them, which they could barely make out in the moonlight.

"Yes, Sir? But what of it?"

"What is made from it?" Craven sighed.

"Wine," smirked Birback.

Paget's eyes were adjusting a little better now, and he could see the little group who looked most suspicious as if they were up to no good.

"What of it? There is no wine here," complained Paget as he looked about at the crops which were merely an ingredient, and he could not understand how it would help them.

"Up here no, but down there," smiled Craven as he pointed towards a chimney rising up from the ground.

"What do you mean?" Paget asked in amazement and curiosity.

"The making of wine in these parts is subterranean."

"And vast," added Vicenta.

"Down that?" Paget looked to the stone chimney.

"Undermining for acres all around and great vats to press the wine," smiled Craven.

"And what, you mean to take some?"

"A little payment for our efforts," smirked Birback.

"You mean to steal from our allies?"

"The locals here fled for their lives from the French, and we now fight to get their lands back. I don't think they'll mind us reaping a little of the rewards," replied Timmerman.

But Paget looked over and into the chimney to see it was entirely dark like a pit.

"Not me," he asserted.

"I will," replied Birback firmly. He began to strip off his weapons and equipment to lighten his descent and ensure he could make the climb back up.

"And if there is one of the winemakers down there?"

"Why would he not be in his bed at this time?" replied Craven.

"We are not," insisted Paget.

But Birback licked his lips as he imagined all of the wine he would enjoy as he took canteens from each of them to sling about his waist.

"If I tug on this rope, you pull me back up, you hear?"

He climbed over the edge as the others took the weight and slack of the rope, and he began his descent as they lowered him slowly. The vault was taller than many houses and so it was a long way down.

"Sir, do the owners of these places not make efforts to protect them?" Paget asked Craven.

"Yes, and they will cut any thieves with their long knives," replied Vicenta.

Craven smiled, but Paget looked mortified.

"Did he take a weapon with him?"

Craven shook his head.

Lower and lower Birback went until he finally touched the ground. Now he was alone and in the dark, the confidence he had exuded above ground quickly evaporated. He realised how dangerous a situation he had potentially entered. His eyes were slowly adjusting to the darkness, but he had to use his hands to navigate. He dared not take a torch down with him and attract the attention of anyone who might be inside. He kept moving forward, feeling his way as he went when one of the canteens knocked into something metallic.

"What's that?" he whispered to himself.

He reached out with his hands and touched the cold clammy face of a corpse. He shuddered a little and recoiled in disgust and horror. The body wore the uniform of a French soldier and had many lacerations from a blade.

"Oh no, no, no," he recoiled quietly, looking around in all directions as if to try and find the assassins which waited in the darkness for the Frenchman, and perhaps now for him. He dared not speak out for chance of attracting them to him, and so he quickly tracked back to where he had been lowered and pulled on the rope violently to be hauled back to the surface.

"Did you get it?" Craven called out with suspicion as he had not been long.

"Just pull me up!" Birback cried in desperation.

He was looking back and forth, swearing at his comrades for the delay as he expected to be attacked in any moment. He was breathing heavily with panic in his eyes. None of his comrades had seen him exhibit such fear, and they couldn't now in the darkness. Finally, the rope around him went taut and he began to be hoisted up. He kept looking down at his feet, expecting some devil to jump out of the abyss and pull him back down. But when he was high enough from the ground that he was confident no man could reach him, he breathed a little relief and began to scramble his way out of the chimney to get out as quickly as possible. He reached the top, hauled himself out, and collapsed over the side onto the flat of his back. He was panting and looked mortified. They could all see his canteens were empty and he looked most agitated. Craven burst into laughter at the sight, as Birback always maintained such a brutish and confident manner about them all and it had been shattered. The others soon joined in as they were greatly enjoying the spectacle.

"There is a dead Frenchman down there, hacked to death by one of the owners, no doubt," protested Birback as he defended himself.

But the explanation only caused them all to laugh even louder at his plight.

"Alright, alright, this is all most enjoyable, but it would be better with wine," declared Timmerman.

He unhooked his sabre and handed it to Craven. He kept the sword belt on, for it carried a large dagger. As brave as he was, he was not going to descend into the darkness empty-handed after the news Birback had brought to them. He looped the rope about him and went down into chimney without hesitation, and this brought them all to silence for some time as they waited and listened for the slightest noise below. Ten minutes went by and there was nothing.

"Do you think he is okay, Sir?" Paget asked.

There was a tug on the rope, and so they got to work. In no time at all Timmerman leapt out from the chimney with a brace of canteens filled to the brim with wine as they sagged heavily about his waist. A cheer rang out as he handed them out amongst the small party and instantly lifted their spirits. Craven lifted up one of the canteens towards Timmerman as if to salute with it, clashing it against the one his old adversary held before they took their fill. Craven handed the canteen on to Paget who initially looked a little uncomfortable at the prospect, but soon took a great gulp.

The next morning, they rode on in good spirits and rendezvoused with Timmerman on the road East as Wellington had ordered, giving them fifty mounted infantry. They could hear the sound of musket and cannon fire in the distance, but a heavy fog clung over the lands in the early hours.

"This way."

Timmerman led them up a hill on the Northern side of the Tormes. They burst through the fog and onto the vantage point where they found Wellington and his entire headquarters staff, having come for the same purpose. Wellington looked back to see Craven approach with a smile.

"They push us, Major. I would push them back!"

He carefully studied his map with a compass, but as he did so, the fog began to lift, and they got a good look with their own eyes. Bock's heavy cavalry of the King's German Legion were retreating across an open plain, but in good order and fighting as they moved, pursued by a significantly larger force of infantry, light cavalry, and horse artillery. Fire was exchanged back and forth as Bock's heavy cavalry were driven back by the French.

"Then enemy look to control the ford at Huerta, there, at the elbow!"

Wellington pointed to a bend in the river several miles to the East where it turned from North to West, towards Salamanca, "Marmont means to spearhead an advance here, and he must be stopped! Send orders for General Graham to cross the Tormes and blunt this enemy attack with the 1st and 7th Divisions, and Le Marchant also."

Craven could see how serious the situation was.

Thousands of French troops were advancing in the distance, and Wellington's large commitment to counter them threatened to escalate into a major battle.

"And me, Sir? What should I do?" Craven asked.

"Support Le Marchant and protect the guns he is bringing up."

"Yes, Sir!"

He raced on with his party towards the Heavy Brigade and met them where they crossed the Tormes to move to support Bock's cavalry. It was a grand operation and did indeed feel like a great battle was about the commence, the one they had all been waiting for.

"Finally, a chance at 'em!" Le Marchant roared.

There was a general excitement amongst them all as they went forward. The horse artillery didn't much appreciate the ragged group of Craven's force that had been sent to support them. For they were finely dressed and proud soldiers, and yet they did not complain. They knew Craven's reputation, and this was not a parade but the beginnings of a battle.

On they advanced until finally drawing up in their positions to face the enemy. There had to be nine or ten thousand French troops marching towards them, and they had formed up battle lines ahead as if to give battle. Being a quarter of Marmont's force, it seemed impossible he would not commit to a larger engagement if he was willing to send such a large force forward, and yet as the British force advanced, the French one withdrew. Both sides took up defensive positions, gazing upon one another just as they had from the heights of San Cristobal. It was a tense moment as it seemed a serious battle was about to commence. The French force withdrew and began to march back for the Huerta ford. Cavalry from both sides exchanged carbine fire as the two forces continued to manoeuvre, but no battle came.

British troops fell back to their defensive positions, and it was stalemate once more. They remained in place overnight, watching and waiting for the French force to move once again. Yet again Marmont had tried to outmanoeuvre the British force, and once again nothing had come of it, but there was little sense of achievement in it. Only a handful of casualties had been inflicted on each side that day and nothing had been gained for either. The next day soon came and yet still the French would not move as Wellington would want them to, and he came to see for himself. He was as frustrated as the rest of the army as he continually set traps which Marmont would not fall into.

"What do you say, Craven?"

Craven was stunned and a little awkward, as there were many officers far superior to him within earshot, but Le Marchant had gathered beside them also and nodded for him to go on.

"One thing at a time, Sir. The forts are our focus and must be overcome. Let us not chase for a battle when that task is not complete, for that is Napoleon's manner of mistake."

"You think so, do you?" Wellington asked curiously.

"Napoleon has a great battle on his hands here in Spain, and if he were to march South and face us, we might be in quite some bother, but instead, he turns his attention to the next target before dealing with the first. A man should always deal with the closest threat at hand before worrying about that which is not within reach."

"Ever the swordsman," Wellington smiled.

"I believe he is right. For there is nothing I should like more than for our lads to get a chance at the enemy, but it would not be proper to press for it until those forts are taken. That operation hangs on to us like a ball and chain, and we must remove it before pressing on."

"And if the enemy presses on?" Wellington was looking towards the defensive French lines that had been established.

"If Marmont meant to attack, he would have done it yesterday. He looks for a weakness, but he finds none," replied Le Marchant.

Wellington seemed to appreciate the cavalry commander's assessment. They spoke as if they were great friends, though it was hardly surprising, for they had both fought in the Low Countries together almost twenty years back.

"Craven?" Wellington asked.

"Yes, Sir."

"These games we play are getting tiresome. You are to carry a message to Salamanca for me. The forts are to be pressed as early and vigorously as possible. Take them, Major. Do whatever you have to do but know that time is our greatest priority now."

"Yes, Sir," he replied.

CHAPTER 12

Paget and Ferreira watched Craven deliver Wellington's news to those besieging the forts. They look upon Craven with despair and frustration as they protested. Craven seemed to be understanding, but they could not hear what he was saying.

"He has come a long way, hasn't he?" Ferreira smiled as he imagined a fight ensuing in times past.

"Haven't we all?"

Craven returned to them looking as exasperated as the Artillery officers and others he had delivered the news to.

"You told them?" Ferreira asked.

"I did, and the guns are in place and ready to continue their work, but they have no ammunition. What are they to do without ammunition?"

He didn't need to say it, as the idle gun crews and relative quiet made the situation quite clear. It was a frustrating one, and so both sides remained idle, with only a few sharpshooters exchanging fire here and there as the day went on. Yet there was still work to be done, but it could not be done in the daylight.

As the sun went down, work parties began to assemble with picks and shovels. They soon went on to expand a trench down along the bottom of the ravine which divided San Vincente and the smaller two forts. When complete, the trench would cut communication from the main fort entirely. It would be one more step in overcoming the powerful structures and give valuable staging posts from where the infantry might make their assaults. The work parties got to it under the protection of darkness, but still the enemy rained down fire wherever they could, killing and wounding several.

It was grim work and kept Paget up for much of another night as he watched from afar. Moxy, Ellis, and several of Ferreira's riflemen stayed up through the night to take well aimed shots at the enemy so as to not give them an easy time of targeting those at work in the trench.

Paget heard a noise behind him and turned with a smile, thinking it was Ferreira once more, but it was Charlie.

"You should get some rest," she insisted.

"Those men cannot. Look at them as they toil away through the night." He was looking towards those hard at work. Many had now gotten into the dead ground where they could not be seen by any of the French soldiers firing from the forts, but still they took shots at every opportunity they could see.

"Do not think you do too little, for that would not be true, not even close to true. A soldier cannot be fighting all of the time."

"But you would, if you could."

"No, I would not. I don't want to fight this war anymore.

I just want to win it," she replied honestly.

"And then? What will you do after it is all over?"

"Go back to England with my friends and live out a life in peace."

"That is truly what you want?"

"It was always what I wanted, only the French stole it from me, or at least that is what I thought for the longest time."

"You don't anymore?"

"No. Fighting and killing the French will not bring back my late husband, nor the joy of those days. I was not really fighting them. I was fighting myself. I thought it would make me feel better, or that it might honour him, but none of that is true. I was angry, and more anger was never going to bring me peace. I can see that now, and I am ashamed to say it has taken me this long. I will go on fighting, but not because I enjoy it, but because peace is worth fighting for. I don't care what our lives are when we go back to England, only that as many of us do make it home as is possible."

"It warms me to hear it, but I fear we are so far off such a day."

"It doesn't matter when it comes, only that it does."

"It has been quite a thing, our time here in Spain and Portugal, hasn't it?" he smiled as he relaxed somewhat.

"It certainly has. Now let's get some rest. We will need it. For those soldiers work by night, and we shall work by day. We must have our strength."

The morning soon came, and once more the guns were silent, for there was no ammunition for it. But the trench dividing the forts was complete, and British pickets now held the position, cutting off the line of communication from the

French headquarters and the strongest of the fortifications, San Vincente. The morning was for a while quiet, until cheers began to echo through the city, and Craven and the others turned out of their shelters to see the cause of it. A column of mules was being led through the streets as far as the eye could see, heavily laden with shot for the cannons and their crews who waited impatiently for them. The supplies were a cause of great celebration for the whole combined British, Portuguese, and Spanish army. They knew it was the turning point they had all been waiting for.

"Come on, boys, let's get these guns going!"

Craven raced to be amongst the first to help unload the vast and heavy supplies, and his comrades did the same. Even Paget joined in as he was overcome by joy at the sight of the ammunition. Within thirty minutes they were all stripped to their shirts and dripping with sweat as they carried the supplies back and forth. Most of the guns were now positioned to bombard San Cayetano, the scene of the disastrous assault from two days past, whilst others took aim at San Vincente. It took several hours of back breaking work to prepare the guns for bombardment and have everything in place, but as the time drew nearer, fires were lit amongst furnaces in the city and steel baskets closer to the gun positions. Paget watched with great intrigue as cannon shot was lowered into one of the metal baskets before ensuring the shell was well covered by the burning hot coals. It was even hotter work than they had put in throughout the day as the gunners toiled in the scorching heat.

"What are they doing?" Joze had never seen the cold iron shot warmed before.

"Making red hot shot," replied Paget who watched on

with great intrigue.

"Red hot shot?"

"They are mostly used at sea for the purpose of burning ships, a most dangerous task," replied Matthys.

"I have read about the practice, but I have never seen it, and I did not know it was used on the land," replied Paget curiously.

"What can fire do against stone?" replied Joze as he looked to the old convents.

"The enemy have used a lot of timber in the fortifying of those places, a great deal of it, and they of course have great powder stores also," replied Craven.

"We mean to burn those forts to the ground?"

"If it can save us another assault like the last one we witnessed, most certainly."

It was a hot day and the work had made it far worse. There was no wind, and the fires and furnaces seemed to double the temperature, and so they remained in their shirts as they waited and watched for the opening salvo. It came in the afternoon at 3 o'clock when the four great eighteen-pounders roared as they lashed out at San Cayetano. Volley after volley was fired, and the results were far better than their first efforts with such little ammunition. Gunners carried the fiery red hot shot to their howitzers, which soon began to target the roof and upper floors of San Vincente. The results were undeniable as fires erupted throughout the day. And by nightfall a great deal of San Vincente was alight as the French soldiers struggled to put out and contain the blazes. Eruptions roared occasionally as some small powder supply went up in flames, and nightfall did not bring peace to the fortifications. For just as the French had fired down on the workers and assaulters for days, now the Royal Artillery pounded the fortifications throughout the night.

There was little sleep to be had under the continual roaring bombardment, and yet through exhaustion and heat most of them managed two hours. It was the middle of the night, and Paget was once again wide awake and watching the nights action continue. Fires raged all across the French fortifications as those inside battled to keep them under control, of which they were so far managing. The artillery fire was unrelenting as the French positions were smashed over and over.

First light soon came, and woodsmoke wafted about the city, as did powder smoke, and still there was no breach. Daylight did not bring any pause for the artillery. If anything, it caused them to up their pace as if angered that the obstacle before them was still standing in defiance of their great efforts. Despite all the fires raging across the three forts, the French guns continued to roar as they targeted the British gun emplacements.

The guns raged for another four hours that morning, and it seemed as if the fires were under control until finally a breach was blasted into San Cayetano. Cries of relief and jubilation rang out amongst the besieging troops. It was a great relief to them all. At the same time, a new and even greater fire had ignited at San Vincente. It began to engulf the entire building with smoke, and finally, the guns there went silent as the crews panicked and struggled to contain the blaze.

Craven pulled on his sword belt, eager to get a chance at the fort. Wellington ordered an assault forward which had been prepared and in waiting all morning to do what must be done. The party moved off for the cover of the trench to make their approach on the breach of San Cayetano as Craven went after them.

"Major?" Wellington asked, as if questioning his advance without orders.

"Yes, Sir?" he replied as he paused briefly.

"Time is what matters most. Do you hear me? Do whatever it takes to end this at the soonest opportunity, do you hear?"

"Yes, Sir."

Craven led his party on, and even Timmerman was with them, eager to be part of the victory. They rushed along the trench in the ravine with almost no resistance and only the odd musket shot levelled at them with clouds of smoke bellowing from San Vincente covering their advance nicely. They got into position as the officer commanding the forlorn hope looked back to Craven with a look of both pride and fear. It was nothing as dangerous as the same event at Badajoz, but that did not diminish the risk and bravery of those who volunteered for it.

"Ready boys?" cried the officer.

"Look, Sir!" Paget yelled.

They looked into the breach. A white flag had been lifted just seconds before the assault was about to be launched. The officer of the forlorn hope looked a little stunned and confused, but finally, he got out of the trench. He climbed the first half of the breach as the Captain of the San Cayetano fort came out with two of his staff to talk with him.

"Stay here," ordered Craven as he went on to join them, and yet Paget followed him anyway.

"What are you doing?" Craven asked as they went forward.

"Seeing this done," he insisted as if he believed it was vital, and he was part of the negotiations if they were to be successful.

As Craven reached the small party, the French and British officers were already deep in conversation, and only stopped briefly as he arrived.

"What do they want?" Craven demanded of the leader of the forlorn hope.

"They request a two-hour truce with which to communicate with their commanding officer in San Vincente, and then they will surrender after that time."

Craven said nothing for a moment as he studied the French officer and his associates. They looked confident, even arrogant, and yet put on a brave face as if they were all friends.

"You have five minutes to march out if you wish to preserve the lives of your men," declared Craven boldly.

Paget was stunned.

"Monsieur, you must understand. We need time to…" began the French officer as he tried to haggle further.

But Craven stepped closer to him. He grabbed hold of the white flag he was holding and tossed it to the ground.

"Five minutes, that is all," he repeated before leading Paget and the other officer back to their trench.

The Frenchman was stunned and yet retreated back into the breach, leaving the white flag on the ground where it had been thrown.

"Are you allowed to do that, Sir?"

"They are stalling, and they have nothing to gamble with. I will not give them two hours to bolster their defences," he replied sternly as he watched the seconds tick down on his pocket watch. Soon enough it was time, and he nodded towards the officer who had volunteered to lead the way. It was time, and they all knew it. Craven drew out his sword and pistol ready for a fight.

"Forward!" cried the leader of the forlorn hope.

They leapt out of the trench and stormed forward. A few musket shots rang out from those French soldiers inside, but they were soon at the breach with little resistance. As they stormed inside, the French soldiers threw down their muskets and offered no further resistance. Cheers rang out as the garrison gave up the fight and those making the assault did so with only a handful of casualties. They took to the walls to celebrate and taunt those in San Vincente, but it was engulfed with such flames as few inside could look out. A white flag now went out from one of the windows. Craven rushed back out from San Cayetano to get a better look as the larger fort still burned. A small party was gathering outside, including what appeared to be the officer in charge.

"Are they done, Sir?" Paget asked.

"Let's find out." Craven stormed on down into the trench which divided them and back up the other side to reach the French party. He approached at the same time as several other officers but leapt in to take the lead before they could.

"I am Governor Duchemin," declared the Frenchman.

"Major Craven."

Duchemin recognised the name, and it gave him a slight pause for concern.

"Major Craven, I request three hours of peace so we might see to our wounded."

"You have five minutes to march everyone out and take your honours of war and your baggage with you. Five minutes," he reiterated just as he had given the same terms at San Cayetano.

"Monsieur Craven, you must understand it will take time to gather all that we must and prepare ourselves…" he went on and kept on talking.

But Craven was done listening as he looked down to see a Company of Caçadores primed and ready to assault. He gestured for them to begin, and then leapt out from the trench and advanced rapidly from the Eastern side of the fort.

"Monsieur, we are under a white flag!" Duchemin protested.

"No, you are wasting my time."

They watched the Caçadores storm in through an open breach unopposed. French soldiers all around them put down their weapons, for there was no will to go on fighting. With the many breaches and fires still raging, it was a forgone conclusion. Soon enough the unarmed French soldiers began to march on out from the ruined fort, nearly six hundred in total. British, Portuguese, and Spanish troops roared at the triumph, though it was also a disheartening sight for how few casualties had been inflicted on the enemy after such a prolonged bombardment.

Yet it did not matter. All that was important was that the French fortifications had fallen. Salamanca was now entirely rid of the French, and any hope of Marmont breaking the siege was over. It was dangerous to both besiege a fortification and protect against a field army at the same time, but now the situation had been simplified greatly. Soldiers all around celebrated loudly, whilst many of the gunners merely sat down and breathed a sigh of relief, utterly exhausted from a lack of sleep and a relentless toll on their minds and bodies.

Wellington approached Craven as the celebrations continued.

"What did you offer them?"

"Five minutes or we'd end 'em."

Wellington looked back to Spring with disbelief.

"Five minutes?" he replied in astonishment and glee.

"The enemy were playing for time, but they had nothing to bargain with."

"Many a man would have given them an hour or two so that they may save their dignity," replied Spring.

"There is no shame in their losing. They put up a most admirable defence, but a man must know when he is done."

"I might agree, but I am not sure you have ever known it yourself," replied Wellington.

"What now, Sir?" Craven smiled at Wellington.

"Marmont will withdraw, for there is nothing for him here now. There is no risk worth taking. He will retire where he is more sure of reinforcement."

"And you, Sir, what will you do?"

"We will give pursuit and attempt to force an engagement upon the enemy whilst we still have the advantage. Matters have not gone as I could wish here, but we still hold the advantage, and now we may press it. Be ready to move out, Craven, for as soon as Marmont begins to withdraw, I want to be on him."

CHAPTER 13

An explosion rang out in the distance, and Craven stormed up onto a small hill to get a good look for himself. A cloud of smoke wafted from the ruins of a bridge which had been blown on a river well ahead of them, well before the British cavalry scouts could reach it. They could see the French columns in the distance and moving at a robust pace.

"Wellington is losing control of the situation," declared Timmerman.

"Take that back," snarled Paget.

"He is not wrong, and he would freely admit it amongst close friends," added Craven.

"Even if it were true, it should not be said," snapped Paget.

"It is worth knowing how things stand, even if it is news which is not comfortable."

Paget growled angrily as he knew what Craven had said to

be true but hated hearing it said aloud.

"What is for it, Sir?"

"All we can do is keep giving chase and hope they turn around and fight us."

"Is that what we want, Sir? To be on the attack? That does not sound much like Sir Arthur."

"It is when he has the advantage in strength, and even now we still have it. More troops, more cavalry, we have never been in such a strong position since it all began, and I am sure Wellington is eager to make best use of it. We need a victory."

"Then we should be on it, Sir. Let us harass them most vigorously until they stop and fight," insisted Paget before riding on to lead the way, not caring to wait for orders.

"He is more and more like you every day," said Timmerman.

"I can't tell if that is a compliment or insult."

"That rather depends on whether you think you are a good man or not."

"Good enough I hope, but he is better than any of us."

"It is a miracle he did not turn out to be a complete bastard, just like me," smiled Timmerman. He then raced on after the Lieutenant.

"How did we ever end up with him?" Ferreira groaned.

"Timmerman? He is an awful enemy to have, and the French know it as well as us. You will be glad of a man like that beside you when all hell is coming at you."

Ferreira shrugged as he knew it was true.

They rode on as the pursuit continued. It was not long before they were at a small river where they were forced to wade across. The bridge was blown to bits, and they could hear musket fire in the distance as the French rear guard fought back all advances. The enemy were doing everything in their power to slow Wellington's advance.

"Will the enemy not stand and fight, Sir?" Paget angrily waded through the deep water, getting his feet wet in the process.

"Not whilst we have the advantage."

They went on up the next gentle slope and stopped atop it to catch a breath as they watch the enemy retreat far into the distance.

"They run like the devil were chasing them," declared Paget.

"Maybe he does," smiled Craven as Timmerman rode up behind them.

"Marmont force marches his army," stated Timmerman.

It must be true, for they were progressing North at an immense pace.

"Will they ever stop, Sir?"

"Not until they have a position favourable to them," admitted Craven.

On and on the pursuit went, day after day, but the French moved quickly. The small skirmishes with the rear guard did not last for long as they continued North at every opportunity, until after many gruelling days they heard Moxy cry out from a vantage point ahead. They hoped something was happening at last.

They rushed on as quickly as they could, though both man and horse were now very weary. As they joined the Welshman, they were met with a most surprising sight. The French army was no longer in flight but spread out for many miles in both directions. Craven took out his spyglass for a better look as he knew something surely must have changed. He soon spotted it as he took out his map to be certain of it.

"The Douro," he declared.

The river's name brought back so many memories.

"The one we crossed at Porto, Sir?" Paget was thinking back to that first great triumph they had enjoyed together so many years ago.

"One and the same," agreed Craven.

"Then they have finally decided to stand against us?"

"Yes, and in a significantly stronger position," sighed Craven.

They watched as both armies spread out along the river, taking up strong positions with a calmness, as if knowing a battle would not come quickly now. And they were right, as nightfall came without any action. Craven was called to Wellington's tent. He took Paget with him, and nobody protested, for the young man's status carried a lot more weight than his lowly rank. They entered to find several others with Wellington, including Spring and Thornhill.

"What is he doing here?" demanded one of the officers who looked down on a Lieutenant being present amongst such senior officers. He gave almost as dirty a look at Craven being only a Major.

"Your father disowned you, and so you are nothing but that uniform now," spat the officer at Paget.

Craven moved a little towards the man as if to strike him.

"Craven!" Wellington roared.

He stopped, though looked hesitant and clenched his fists, but Wellington took on his opponent for him.

"Mr Paget is one of the finest officers in this damned army, and his father is a fool. But more importantly, how dare you speak in such a tongue in my presence! You have your orders, so get out, Colonel."

The officer looked quite sheepish and left without another word.

"Thank you, Sir," said Paget.

"No, I am sorry for such stupidity in all of our presence. I will not have this bickering amongst my officers. Leave it to the French!"

"Yes, Sir," smiled Craven.

"That goes for you, too, Major. This dispute with Colonel Blakeney must end, for all our sakes."

"It was not of my doing, Sir."

"I don't care why, only that it stops."

"Yes, Sir," he agreed.

"Now, onto why I brought you here." Wellington pointed at a map hung on a board beside him, "The enemy spread out across the riverbank here. There are several crossings but none of them may be made quickly or easily by a sizeable force."

"Then whoever attacks first is at a massive disadvantage?"

"Indeed, Mr Paget. I pursued Marmont North because I hoped to force him into battle, whilst he retired further and further as he waits on reinforcements from both Bonet and Cafferelli. I am willing to gamble both will stay in the North as per Napoleon's orders."

"Even if Marmont appeals to them directly for assistance?"

"Yes, but I do not rely on hope alone. Through the last few weeks and for many more there are a great many plans unfolding which we will not see nor hear, but they are happening. Guerrillas are coming down from their mountain fortresses. The Royal Navy is striking at the Northern coast of Spain. The last armies of Spain are marching also. Everywhere pressure is being placed on the French so that they will be unable to move, unable to communicate, and fearful of leaving their posts."

"And so Marmont will receive no reinforcements?" Craven asked.

"That is correct, and so now we wait for him to decide whether he will take a risk and make an attack on us, or retreat further, and he will not outrun us again."

"And if he does neither, Sir, and he stays where he is?"

"Cavalry and militia move to ensure his soldiers cannot forage freely. We have cut off most of his communications and supply lines, whilst we get a ready supply through Portugal. Time is not on Marmont's side."

Craven breathed a sigh of relief as it seemed as though everything was in hand.

"You are most valuable to me out there on edge of things as my eyes but also as a perpetual thorn in the enemy's side. Continue your work, Craven, and let us see this through."

"Yes, Sir."

He left with an excitable Paget by his side, and yet it was obvious to the Lieutenant that he did not share his enthusiasm.

"What is it, Sir?"

"More waiting. More uncertainty," he groaned as he went to find their camp.

Wellington's army had spread out over a great many miles across the river, so that it would take a day's march to assemble it again. It was the only means with which to cover all of the passes so that Marmont could not push one of the flanks. As night came, they watched as the enemy settle around their fires on the North side of the river whilst they did the same on the South side. Both armies kept well back from the river so as to not be in danger of enemy fire, but close enough that they could make a dash for the embankments if need be. The occasional picket wandered close to the water in order to keep an eye on the other side, but it was to be a peaceful night as far as all could see.

"Still, we wait. That is all we ever do," protested Paget.

"There is a great deal more going on here than merely waiting. Each side tests the other and looks for an opening. We must remain vigilant, for the enemy will most certainly test us at every opportunity."

But he could see they were all just as tense as Paget, and he knew he must try to calm their nerves so that they may sleep as best they could and be capable and ready for anything.

"Joze, gather the singlesticks."

"Yes, Sir."

"You would fight, Sir? Now?" Paget asked.

Matthys smiled as he knew precisely what Craven was doing and why, and yet there was little enthusiasm for it.

"Joze, do you think you can take on a competent swordsman now?" Matthys asked.

"I have killed my fair share."

"Not with a knife in the back or at the throat, in a fair fight," replied Paget.

Craven looked to Matthys who wore an amused expression, knowing he was in on the game as he riled them up.

It was a challenge and a contest which would get them all fired up.

"Well, will you rise to the occasion?" Paget demanded as if his honour had been put into question.

"Of course."

Joze smiled as he happily agreed and took a singlestick for himself. He threw the other to the ground before Paget, which the Lieutenant did not appreciate. It was evidently all part of his plan. Paget cursed at the gesture before stripping away his sword belt in readiness. He was already angry, and yet Joze was as calm as could be. Craven gestured towards Matthys to conduct and oversee the contest.

"The first man to three smart blows is the victor. Have a good contest, gentlemen," declared Matthys.

"Gentlemen?" Paget spat instinctively, reverting to his old ways as if he was a boy once more and looking down on a peasant.

"Begin!"

Only a dozen of the Salford Rifles were watching, but Joze began to tap his stick against Paget's with short sharp beats. The crack of hardwood beating together drew many more eyes and soon enough they had a sizeable crowd. Joze was still smiling as he tapped against Paget's stick, for he could see it was annoying him, and that only made him continue until he had done it a dozen times. Paget finally responded and snapped a quick beat in himself as if to launch into an attack, but Joze lowered his own stick. Paget's found nothing but air, and he ended up looking at the tip of his opponent's weapon, which was now directed towards him and threatening his face. He was frustrated further as Joze had used a common strategy against him, one he had known since his days fencing the foil, and now he was not only angry with his opponent, but also angry with himself.

And yet despite Joze's characteristic fencing move, he did not hold himself like a fencer. His hilt was low and protracted, and he shook his singlestick up and down in what seemed to be a predictable rhythm. Paget tried to take advantage of it and launched a thrust into the movement as the tip of the stick swayed back and forth. But Joze beat down against his stick and leapt past Paget, slapping him in the ribs as he did so. Paget could barely believe what had happened. The blow did not hurt his body, only his pride. He winced angrily and dropped his head in shame for a moment.

"Come on, Lieutenant!" Charlie roared.

It was enough to spur him on as he came back to guard. Joze circled him like a wild animal stalking his prey, but he knew he was letting the situation get away from him. He was better than this, and he knew it. He went forward and launched several feints. When Joze tried to traverse out to his side again, he flew back with a jump and tapped Joze on the top of the head with a short sharp stroke. It was not even enough to draw blood, but that was intentional.

A little cheer rang out as the crowd was enjoying it now. But Joze came forward again, without any footwork which would resembling fencing and more like a wrestler. He snapped cuts from one side to another with rapid succession, rotating only from the wrist and striking just like a cudgel player would, who were renowned for their speed if not their wealth of knowledge of the sword. Paget parried off every blow, but Joze had gotten so close with his aggressive footwork that when he struck down towards his lead leg, he could not slip it in time and felt the singlestick slash across both of his thighs. A cheer rang out as the crowd was loving it, but Paget was not amused.

They came back to guard once more, and this time he went on the attack with a flurry of skilful feints and short strikes, finally traversing off to Joze's right side and striking at the back of his knee. It caused the leg to buckle a bit so that when Joze was about to topple over, Paget struck a smart blow down on his nose. It sent him crashing to the ground and achieved him victory. The audience was quiet for a moment as it was a display of savagery from Paget. There was an expectation between gentlemen and fencers more widely that one would stop after each blow landed and pause for a moment before continuing. Yet Paget had carried on as if it were a real contest for life and limb. Joze coughed a little as he got up and blew some blood out of his nose. Everyone hung on his response, for men had challenged others to duels for less. Finally, he began to laugh out loud and went over to Paget to offer a hand in friendship and appreciation for his skill. Paget did not know how to respond, but the crowd loved it as they cheered, and Paget was compelled to accept.

"A fine contest, who is next!" Matthys called out.

The mood was lifted well, but the next days brought only boredom and tension as they carried out scouting duties and waited for enemy responses only for nothing to come of any of it. They were all now as weary as Paget with it, and yet after a week they could see a column of dust to the North, and they knew what that meant.

"The reinforcements Wellington said would not come?" Paget asked.

"If only a half of what Marmont called on have come he

will equal us in the field," replied Craven.

But nothing changed, for neither side was willing to take any great risks. The river between them was a great defensive feature that was holding everyone back. Over a week went by since the French numbers swelled and still nothing.

"It's happened, Sir. It's happening!" Paget cried.

Craven was shaken awake from where he was sleeping under a tree on a warm afternoon. The prospect of any change was a welcome one, and he shot up from his slumber.

"Where? What is happening?"

"The French, Sir, they are moving West!"

"That can only mean one thing."

"They mean to cross? They mean to do battle?"

Riders soon materialised as the orders for Wellington's army were given out to move on. Craven and the others went with the army as they began to shuffle West, mirroring the enemy's drive in that direction. But soon enough the sun was going down once more and no battle had begun, and no attempt at crossing had been made. Fires were lit yet again as everyone settled in for the evening, but Timmerman approached looking most uncomfortable.

"What is it?" Craven asked.

"Something isn't right. I have been North of the river and that is not the entirety of Marmont's force, not even close to it."

"You crossed over?"

"The front is fifteen miles long or more. There are more than enough openings to see for oneself."

"Where are the rest? Where are the rest of Marmont's soldiers?" Paget demanded.

Timmerman shrugged.

"Ferreira, you are in command, anyone else who can ride, on me," he ordered. Nobody appreciated setting out as the sun went down, but they were still quite fresh, and nobody questioned it. They were mostly just excited that something was happening, or at least it appeared as though it was. They rode on Eastward and soon enough discovered masses of cavalrymen preparing to ride out just as they had.

"What news? Where are you going?" Craven asked.

But nobody would answer. For they either did not know or they would not share it without the permission of their superiors. Yet soon enough he spotted Le Marchant assembling troops and seeing to their readiness.

"Sir, what is this?" He rode up beside the General.

"We are undone, we are tricked. Marmont's force changed direction a full day past, and they have crossed to the East. They move to threaten our flanks, and even our rear. I do not know how many men Marmont has crossed with, but we must reach the rear guard at Castrejon. Wellington rides on now with two brigades of cavalry as he currently prepares."

"May we ride with you, Sir?"

"I would welcome it, but I would ask you go ahead and find Lord Wellington. He rides for Castrejon, and he may travel more quickly than we can manage all these men."

There was panic in Le Marchant's voice. It was well concealed as Craven was accustomed to doing himself but was plain to see and hear.

"Protect Wellington, for without him I fear we will not win this campaign."

"I will see it done," replied Craven earnestly as he rode on into the dying light.

He had just fifty horsemen by his side, and they were not cavalry, but they could move much faster and with more flexibility than larger formations.

"This cannot be good," said Timmerman.

"What do you mean?" Craven asked

"That the initiative has been seized and Wellington is no longer in control of this situation."

Paget was horrified, but he merely patted Augustus as he hoped for the best and rode on into the night. After several hours they found a small party of riders, a few of whom turned back to oppose them with pistols and swords, but Craven approached without fear or weapon in hand to find Wellington himself with a pistol in hand.

"Major Craven," he gasped in relief, "How do you find yourself in both the very best and very worst of places?"

"General Le Marchant sent me, Sir. We will see you safely to your destination."

"My gratitude, then let us be on. For dark tidings are ahead, and I would see them with my own eyes."

They rode on through the night, though they could not keep a particularly fast pace. For they had some distance to travel, and the lack of light made it dangerous to both horse and rider. There would be no sleep or rest this night, but not one of them needed it. The anticipation and fear of what they would find the next day caused adrenaline to course through their bodies.

At seven in the morning, they arrived at a scene of complete chaos. The French rained down fire on British positions with horse artillery and advanced with both cavalry and infantry. The numbers before them were stunning as the

British light cavalry fought a hard rear guard action as they were being pushed back. Wellington quickly studied the scene and was speechless. A vast French force had managed to cross the Douro without their knowledge and now threatened to roll up their flank, cutting them off from the road to Salamanca entirely.

"Cavalry!" Paget cried.

French light horse burst out from a nearby wood and made a charge for them as if to target Wellington directly. Moxy shot one down and several others opened fire with their rifles, but there was no time to reload as the enemy raced towards them. Craven looked to Wellington in horror, knowing he could be the cause of Wellington's demise if he could not defend his life.

"Salfords to the front!" He took out the sabre Le Marchant had gifted him. He wrapped the sword knot about his wrist and let the sword dangle from it and took out his pistol. He fired as the enemy closed, making sure he had enough time to take up his sword. Timmerman took out a five-barrelled duckbill pistol and fired as the enemy closed, striking three down. Wellington and his staff, including Beresford drew out their swords in readiness to defend themselves, a desperate measure which no army commander would ever wish for. It meant the plan and progress of a battle had gone very badly indeed.

The two sides clashed as cold steel struck cold steel and a melee ensued. The French outnumbered them but were struggling to break through the strong defences of the well-trained riflemen, who were a lot more than they appeared.

"We can't hold them back!" Paget ran one through, only to almost lose his head as he ducked under a sabre blow.

Craven felt a sabre slash over his left arm and knew it was true. He peered around for any way they might escape before the enemy reached Wellington and all was lost. As he did so, he caught a glimpse of a magnificent sight. Bock and Le Marchant's heavy cavalry brigades burst out from the roads behind them and galloped on at full tilt to relieve them.

"It's Le Marchant!"

The sight of the heavies galloping forward in the morning light was a magnificent sight. They felt the thunder of the heavy horses shaking the ground beneath them. The French cavalry officers cried out for their men to retreat, and they were soon in flight, the British and German heavies in pursuit and the Salfords crying out to cheer them on.

Wellington breathed a sigh of relief as he sheathed his sword, having come to close to having to use it in anger, but as he looked out at the chaos behind, he felt his heart sink, and they could all see it.

"It is done. We are done. We were tricked. We were tricked well. Retreat, that is all we can do now, a full retreat back to Salamanca. We will fight them all the way back, but this is their day."

"And we will have ours, Sir," insisted Paget.

"Yes, yes we will," agreed Wellington.

But it was a bitter turn of events. They were forced to turn around and give up all the ground they had taken without having achieved anything, and now they were the ones being pursued.

CHAPTER 14

"Wait for it, wait!" Craven hunkered down amongst the crops beside a road. They could both hear and feel the thunder of horses' hooves drawing nearer. He raised up a little to get a better view as he cocked the lock of his rifle ready to rain down fire. A rider came into view with four others close behind.

"They are not French," said Matthys.

"Hold," replied Craven.

They watched as five ragged-looking riders made haste along the road before them. They wore a mix of soldier's equipment and civilian attire and were covered in dust. They were travelling at high speed and had been on the road for some time. They looked like Spanish guerrillas, but it made no sense that they would be on the roads near the two armies in plain sight. A few moments later a mass of French cavalry came into view giving pursuit.

"Who are they, Sir?" Paget asked as he looked at the ragtag

bunch fleeing from the enemy.

"No idea, but if the enemy want them that badly I want to know why. Get ready."

The fleeing party roared past them. Craven nodded towards Moxy to take the first shot. He fired and struck down the lead officer of the French cavalry, and it was also the signal for everyone to follow him. A sporadic volley erupted, and many of the French cavalrymen were knocked from their horses, but rifles seemed rather overkill here. They were so close the flames of burning powder and cartridge singed many of the Frenchmen who came to a quick halt. Yet those they were pursuing did also. They began pulling pistols from their saddles and rained fire into the enemy. Each one seemed to carry three or four and kept drawing and firing. Craven drew out his sword and stormed out of the cover of the crops. He rushed on at the French cavalry with the other bursting out with blades in hand to support him. The Frenchmen looked horrified and turned their horses about as quickly as they could. They raced away to save their lives as Moxy hurried to reload so he could get off another shot.

"Leave them!" Craven turned back to the mysterious riders who they had saved. Vicenta approached them before anyone could get a word in and spoke with them in Spanish.

"What are they saying?"

"I think they want to deliver a message to Wellington, or…"

"Or what?"

"Major Thornhill," declared one of the men clearly for all to hear.

"How do you know that name?" Craven demanded.

The man understood well enough but replied in Spanish.

"He says the Major provides them with weapons, and in return they provide information of French troop movements and any messengers they intercept. They return to the Major now with important information taken from the enemy."

"They would risk their lives out here in the light of day this close to the whole of Marmont's army to deliver something to us?" Craven asked, suspicious of them.

Vicenta took his concerns to them.

"He says he wants to see the English crush the armies of France, and that this information he holds is important."

Craven turned back to Matthys to look for some advice.

"What do you think?"

"I believe them, and they do not pose any threat to us. If we take them to the Major and their story is true, then we may gain some important information."

"And if it is a lie?"

"Then they will have nowhere to run or escape."

Craven sighed as he still wasn't sure.

"Tell them I am Major James Craven, and I will deliver whatever it is they have to Major Thornhill."

"No!" snarled the Spaniard firmly.

Craven looked at a satchel hanging from the man's saddle. It was clearly of French military origin and looked to be the sort written orders might be convoyed in. He was resting one hand over the strap from which it hung, as if to protect an object of great value.

"And if I choose to take it for myself?"

Vicenta did not have time to translate as the Spaniard replied.

"You would take from a friend?" he replied in a thick

accent, and yet clearly with a solid grasp of English.

The Spaniard had thick black stubble and a swarthy face from years in the bright sun. There was a confidence and arrogance about him, and yet it seemed to be warranted. He did not appear to be a man to be trifled with, and when he had turned back to fight, he had done so with ferocity.

"I do not have any friends out here."

Craven had never spent enough time this far North to meet many of the locals, and especially the local guerrillas.

"But you are a friend to others like me, Major Craven."

Craven looked impressed that the Spaniard was so well informed.

"Any man willing to fight against the French can be a friend of mine. I fight beside some men who I used to despise and want to see dead," he admitted.

Timmerman laughed as it was certainly true.

"Tell me, what is it you have there?"

"Information of French troop advances."

"We know they are advancing. They are chasing us, which is why we march South."

"Not Marmont's army, but those who march to join him."

Craven was surprised, and he could not hide it as he looked to Matthys for a second thought, but Matthys merely shrugged as he had no idea whether they should trust them.

"Vicenta, do you trust them?"

"What do you care what this woman thinks?" demanded the Spaniard.

"That woman will put you in your grave if you keep on with that tongue," snapped Paget.

The Spaniard smiled back.

"Well? Do you?" Craven asked Vicenta.

"No, I do not, but they might be useful," she admitted.

Craven groaned as thought about it.

"If there is any chance this man is telling the truth we must see those documents safely to Major Thornhill," whispered Paget.

"And if they are merely bandits fleeing a patrol?" Timmerman replied.

"Then you can loot their belongings when they are put under arrest."

Timmerman looked most pleased with that, for the men were well armed with some high-quality captured weapons from the French.

"What is your name?" Craven asked the Spaniard.

"Francisco Mateos, but you can call me Mateo."

"And you fight with us?"

"I fight against the French," he replied honestly.

"I will take you to Major Thornhill, but if he does not know you as you say, it will not end well for you, do you understand?"

"Yes."

"Then come with us," he replied just as their horses were brought up and those the enemy had left behind were rounded up. They were not just highly valuable to Wellington's army but robbing the enemy of them was even more so. For they struggled more than ever to find horses to equip their cavalry regiments, and everyone knew it.

"Let's be on our way. The enemy press us at every turn, and all that powder expended could have been heard by anyone."

They rode on and soon passed the British light infantry providing a rear guard as the army progressed back to Salamanca. Nobody attempted to stop Craven and his party as they approached Wellington's headquarters, knowing they would likely find Thorny there. Craven kept a keen eye on the Spaniards, as he was still suspicious of them and knew that travelling with him was giving them unprecedented levels of access to the headquarters of the army. He was alert at all times with a hand near his pistol should it be required. And yet all fears quickly faded away when Thornhill stepped out from the tent and approached with a smile.

"Mateo!"

Craven breathed a sigh of relief and relaxed rather.

"This man says he has important news, captured from the enemy."

"Let us see it, then!" Thorny declared enthusiastically.

Mateos tossed him the satchel. Thorny tore it open and quickly thumbed through the papers inside. A look of deep concern came over his face as he turned and rushed back into Wellington's tent.

"Stay here," ordered Craven as he leapt from his horse and ran on in after the Major.

Wellington looked a little vexed by his sudden arrival but said nothing as he focused his attention on the documents Thornhill had handed him.

"What does it say, Sir?"

"Do you speak or even read French, Major?"

"I do not, Sir."

"Well, I do, for I studied in France many years ago, a skill I must admit is far more useful to me today than I ever realised it would be as a young man."

"Yes, Sir."

"It says King Joseph marches from Madrid with fourteen thousand soldiers. He means to support Marshal Marmont here against us," lamented Wellington.

"And if he manages to join up with Marmont?"

"Then we will face an army far larger than our own, for we are currently equal to Marmont," replied Thornhill.

"This changes nothing at present, for we must continue South," added Spring.

"Indeed, but if we cannot force an engagement in the coming days, then the chance will be lost," declared Wellington.

"Marmont may not have this information," replied Thornhill.

"I suspect not. His communications are severed at every opportunity, just as was the case here. I imagine he will not know for several more days, and so for now he does not know the strength he might have in the future."

"Then we should turn about and fight him, Sir," insisted Craven.

"I wish that we could, but we cannot risk it, for a victory at a high cost could be a defeat in the coming weeks and months. We need a victory of such a decisive nature or no engagement at all."

"That is a lot to ask, perhaps you aim too high, Sir."

Wellington sat back and sighed as he glared at the Major.

"I aim too high? Craven, I wonder if you really understand anything about running a war. You are a fine swordsman and a good officer in the field. Were we to ever duel I have no doubt you would be the victor, but in matters of strategy for an army and a larger war, perhaps it is I who knows more, do you not think?" he replied in a remarkably calm fashion.

"I meant no disrespect, Sir, but the army is eager for a fight, and sometimes the right moment to strike is not always the moment you had hoped and waited for."

"That might be true, but we are not at that stage yet, Major. The next few days will be vital."

"You hope to take the heights at Salamanca once more?"

"What if I do?"

"Begging your pardon, Sir, but Marmont would not attack when you wanted him to last time we were there, why would it be any different a second time?"

"Marmont has been begging for troops from all over Spain, and now he has them, an army with which he finally believes he can crush us," replied Spring.

"He would be a fool to attack us there. He must remember Bussaco and Fuentes, the same as the rest of us. You are gambling on him being a fool?"

"Major, what was it you said just now, 'sometimes the right moment to strike is not always the moment you had hoped and waited for'. Marmont pursues us now because he wants to fight, and if he has not heard of Joseph's advance he will take the moment, because it is the best one he will ever get, as far as he knows," replied Wellington.

"I hope so, Sir, for we made a step forward here in Spain and now it seems we make two backward."

"That will be all, Major," declared Wellington as he had heard enough.

"Yes, Sir," grumbled Craven.

He left and went to Mateo, now relieved to know he was

indeed a friend, or at least an ally. Behind him mules were being loaded with weapons and cartridge boxes, payment for their services.

"The information that you just delivered, have you read it?"

"I have," admitted Mateo without hesitation.

"Then you know its importance. Tell me, do you think Marmont knows this information? Could any other messengers have gotten to him?"

"I very much doubt it, for they are too valuable a target for us. We take from them horses and weapons and anything else of value, and we are paid doubly by your Wellington. A French army might march through my country, but anything less is prey for us."

It wasn't much to go on as he sighed at the prospect of what they were facing.

"You worry your Wellington will not stand and fight?"

Craven said nothing but he could not deny it.

"My men have sometimes said the same about me, but there is something Wellington and I have in common."

"There is?"

"One mistake, one over commitment to a situation which is more than I can overcome, and it could be the end for my men. And it is the same for him. You English did not fight all these years here to merely go home without finishing the job. Wellington waits to choose the moment, and you should trust in him."

"Do you?"

"Yes, and so should you."

Craven sighed and shrugged, knowing it to be true.

"Good luck out there."

"And to you, my friend."

They parted ways as Craven led his party on to find the rest of the Salford Rifles as they settled in for another night on the road. They soon found them in good spirits, with fires lit and good conversation echoing out. It had been a tedious time, but there was a sense that the battle was close, now that the stalemate at the Douro had been broken.

"What did he say to you, Sir? The Spaniard," Paget asked.

"He said I should trust in Wellington. That he would take the risk when the time was right."

"A wise man," smiled Paget.

"But will he? Wellington has fought so many defensive victories because the French just keep coming at us, but now they show caution and do not fall into those traps. We must draw them into battle, and to do so we must take risks."

"I imagine it is quite taxing putting your fate in the hands of others."

"Yes, it is," groaned Craven.

"I was speaking of Wellington."

"Oh?"

"Sir Arthur may lead this army, but he must put his faith in all of us to do what must be done. Every day he depends on so many different men who might fail him in so many different ways. He cannot choose to fight a battle like you do, Sir."

Craven groaned as Paget had turned the tables on him, but most frustratingly he knew the Lieutenant was right, and so he had to concede defeat.

"I fear you would support Wellington's decisions no matter what they were," he retorted.

"Because he has given me good reason to place my trust in him. It is earnt, just as it is for you and I."

"Who taught you such wisdom?"

"You did, Sir, you did," admitted Paget honestly.

Craven took a deep breath and relaxed. He appreciated Paget's sentiment, even if it wasn't entirely true.

At first light the army was quickly on the move so as to not allow Marmont to overrun them. It felt eerily reminiscent of their pursuit of the French, only now the roles were reversed. The two armies continued on in parallel, sometimes closing within one thousand yards and close to rifle range to a skilled marksman, but Wellington had no intention of stopping. For five days the chase went on with only minor skirmishes. It was a gruelling march, with neither side truly wanting to commit to battle. And both attempting to outmanoeuvre the other as they tried to make best use of the defensive positions around the rivers and streams close to Salamanca.

Finally, Wellington's army reached the San Cristobal heights South of Salamanca and once again took up a defensive position. It halted the enemy advance, but it had been exhausting, and it seemed as though all hope of doing battle had been lost as they settled in for another miserable night. Although at least the slopes they occupied were well wooded so they might fuel their fires.

"Will it ever happen, Sir?" Paget now began to doubt it himself.

"A fight is coming, I can smell it," replied Timmerman.

They could see the enemy in the distance. Some artillery pieces were even in range, but no shots were exchanged. Once again, they were to sleep in battle order and without any shelter.

It was an existence the Salford Rifles had become accustomed to, having spent so much time in the wilderness and across the frontier.

"I can smell something, alright," replied Craven.

"Really, Sir?" Paget asked hopefully.

"A storm is coming," replied Matthys.

Paget sunk down in despair, as that was the last thing any of them wanted on the exposed hillsides where they had to remain. A crack of thunder rolled out across the hills, shaking the ground beneath their feet. Then a great flash of lightning lit up the sky. Rain began to pour down upon them as they wrapped themselves in the coats and blankets which they carried, and they huddled about their fires. The rain began to crash down even more violently as the thunder continued to roar, and lightning stuck several trees a few hundred yards away. It was an almighty storm, which terrified man and beast. The fires were expunged by the torrential downpours as the panic of horses ran out between the rolling thunder, which drew Paget's attention. He rushed to their horses and to Augustus, who looked a little shaken but remained stoic as other animals around him panicked.

"I've got you, my friend, I've always got you." He wrapped an arm about Augustus' neck and leant in against him as others tried to calm down the rest of the horses.

Craven and many others remained huddled about their fires though there was no heat left. They could not bring themselves to move until Major Thornhill pushed in between him and Matthys.

"Bloody rough evening, ey?"

"Indeed, what news?" Craven asked.

"Wellington ordered the baggage train back to Rodrigo, and so it seems this is all over. Over before it truly got started," he replied as if amused by the futility of it all whilst really masking his disappointment.

"Our great advance into Spain, and we will leave again without a fight?"

"There is nothing more for it. Neither Marmont nor Wellington will attack until they see a great opening. One great chance for a decisive victory, and neither will give that opening to the other."

"Then that is it? Tomorrow, we march for Portugal once again?"

"It would seem so, but the army remains intact, and that is what matters. No battle is better than a defeat, or even a victory that we cannot recover from."

But that was no relief to Craven.

"Bloody hell!" He got to his feet and threw off his wet blanket as he stomped back towards Wellington's headquarters.

"You are not going with him?" Matthys asked of Thornhill.

"Oh, no, I merely made the spark. The fire will now sustain itself."

Thorny smiled mischievously as if his plan had worked precisely as expected. Matthys appreciated the calculation as they both watched Craven trudge angrily across the sodden ground. His greatcoat became soaked through, only fuelling his fury more. He soon reached Wellington's position to find that no tents had been assembled. They slept out in the rain with the rest of the army. Wellington himself was huddled in his cloak and resting against his saddle on the ground. Craven went up angrily to him and ripped back the cloak to find Wellington gazing back up in disbelief.

"What is the meaning of this?"

Several soldiers nearby moved to accost him, including the Sergeant Major whose first responsibility was Wellington's safety, but Craven turned back and gazed upon him, clenching his fists ready for a fight, and not even needing to go for a weapon.

"It's alright, alright, I say!" Wellington cried as he pulled the cloak back over his shoulders and sat upright to hear what Craven had to say.

"You mean to retreat?"

"I mean to do whatever must be done."

"Don't let this opportunity run away from us."

"What opportunity? Marmont is strong, and so are we. Neither side will risk an assault against such strength."

"Then present weakness."

Wellington looked puzzled, but Craven went on to explain.

"Marmont is looking for his opportunity. He is looking for a weakness, so give him one. Rumour of the retreat is already spreading amongst the army, and it may even reach Marmont by morning, for I am sure he has his spies the same as us. Make us look weak. Make it look as though we are ready to run. Lower your guard and invite an attack."

"Is that what you would do against a strong opponent?"

"Against one I was confident in defeating, yes, I most certainly would," he replied sharply.

"Is that all?"

"It is," replied Craven sternly.

"Let us see what the morning brings, Major."

"Yes, Sir."

"And, Major."

"Yes, Sir?"

"Thank you. You may not be right, and frequently you are not, but I would rather a good officer spoke his mind with confidence than hold his tongue when it mattered."

"I'll hold my tongue when I'm dead."

Wellington chuckled as he relaxed a little, despite the rain pouring down his face.

CHAPTER 15

Craven, like many others, was up early, for everyone knew it would not be a quiet nor easy day. There was a feeling that Wellington's army was about to either march into battle, or retreat towards Portugal; a move which would need to be rushed as to not be caught out by the French army who would undoubtedly pursue them relentlessly. Either way, it was a stressful time. The one saving grace was the change in the weather, for the violent storms of the night had given way to a hot sunny morning which was rapidly drying out the ground and the sodden uniforms of the troops.

"A single division, Sir?" Paget looked out to the East. It was all who were formed up to oppose the enemy, whilst the rest of the army was formed up on the reverse slopes and woodland, hidden from view from the enemy. It was a great advantage. They could see the French army below whilst Marmont could not see Wellington's army. Not its strength nor its manoeuvres. Craven smiled, for he knew Wellington had taken his advice, though he hardly felt as though he could take credit.

"When you fight a man with sword in hand, why do you offer them a target? Why would you lower your sword? Why would you feign inexperience?"

"To lull them into a sense of strength, to invite an attack," replied Paget confidently as he finally understood, "He means to draw the enemy into an attack?"

"Indeed."

"Well, it looks as though it is working." Paget pointed to enemy troops that were advancing.

The enemy were pushing towards Wellington's left flank. The army was formed up in a great L shape to the Southeast of Salamanca. The river Tormes protected to the North and the left flank of the army who were situated at a high altitude amongst open plains. The view before them was dominated by two large hills which looked much like the old iron age hill forts in England.

"I fear we should have secured both of those, Sir."

"The Greater and Lesser Arapile. Yes, I would quite agree on most other occasions, but remember what must be done here. The feint must be sold well."

"That might help." Moxy pointed to the West where the warm morning weather had caused a great dust cloud to rise.

"I don't understand, Sir?"

"Last night we heard that Wellington's baggage train is to withdraw. Think about it." He smiled as he looked back down the slopes to where they could see French divisions coming into view, "A single division is all that the enemy can see, and yet there is movement to our rear? What might the enemy think?"

"That a rear guard is protecting a withdrawal?"

Craven nodded in agreement.

"And it will work?"

"That remains to be seen. All we can do is set traps and see what our opponents do against them."

All they could do now was watch as the French light troops poked and prodded to try and find a weakness, whilst the rest of the army did not commit. On the Northern most flank of Wellington's army a great skirmish had broken out, but it went on and on without any significant movement. They watched and listened to the battle rage on for several hours. The air was thick, and not just from the blistering heat but from the tension felt by all.

"Today we stand on a knife's edge," declared Paget.

"Yes, one last chance to make a difference here. Either we break the enemy here today and show we were right to push into Spain, or we turn our backs and look like fools as we scurry back to Portugal."

Paget was shivering with a mix of excitement and dread as they watched the skirmishes unfold far in the distance, wondering if anything more would come of it. The acrid smell of powder smoke wafted across the hills. The action was so close they could smell and taste it, and yet it was far enough away that they could not feel like they were a part of it.

"I cannot bear it, Sir."

"Stand firm, we will get our moment."

"Will we, Sir?"

"We have to."

But Paget was not convinced. They all needed it, but that

did not mean it would happen. They could see Wellington riding back and forth as he assessed the scene, but this was not a battle. The skirmishes were little more than that, as each side tussled with one another to get some small advantage, whether perceived or real. There was frustration in the Commander's face, for he felt it more than any of them. The whole campaign of 1812 hinged on this moment. All which had been gambled and sacrificed at Ciudad Rodrigo and Badajoz was to earn the chance they had here today. It was an immense sense of pressure placed upon them all, but the anticipation of the battle which could come was also of great excitement to everyone. And yet few would let themselves get their hopes up so soon, only to be shattered by another withdrawal, just that had happened time and time again in the passing weeks. Whether it was instigated by Wellington or Marmont, the end result was much the same. And yet this time it was different. Every soldier knew that if battle could not be made now, a retreat would not be a minor manoeuvre, but a retreat all the way to the border of Portugal.

"Sir, look!" Paget cried.

They were all on edge, and the prospect of some sign of action drew all eyes. French soldiers were beginning to appear from some woodland on a hill south of the Greater Arapile. Wellington noticed it, too, as he galloped back and forth delivering his orders. In no time at all a large body of Caçadores moved quickly towards the enemy to reach the summit before them.

"Will you let your countrymen go it alone?" Craven called to Ferreira, who was surrounded by many more of the Portuguese soldiers of the Salford Rifles. All of them were on foot, their horses having been taken safely to the rear and overseen by Joze.

"Certainly not!"

"Give the order, then, Captain," added Craven as he gave the honour to his friend.

"Avançar!" Ferreira called them to advance.

The Salford Rifles went forward as one at a quick pace, moving to support the Caçadores. It was a proud moment for Ferreira, which he would not forget. He looked to Craven with a thankful expression. The Caçadores ahead were scrambling up to the summit and firing as they went, but the enemy got there first and began to pour fire down upon them. Both the Caçadores and Salford Rifles went down to the ground as they fired and reloaded several times over, picking their shots carefully whilst the French fired more often but with none of the precision. Casualties were low, but progress was not being made and after several minutes Craven was frustrated by it.

"We have to push on!"

The officers of the Caçadores were of the same mind and had already ordered their men to fix their sword bayonets as they prepared to charge.

"Yes!" Craven excitedly slung his rifle over his back and took out his double-barrelled pistol and his sword, the straight bladed Andrea Ferrara that had served him so well. He had left his cavalry sabre upon his saddle, it being a handful when on foot, especially with its huge heavy iron scabbard.

They pushed on up, making a charge for the summit, but the enemy fire was intense. Craven felt burnt wadding scorch his face, and a number of soldiers around him were hit. They pushed on, and yet more Frenchmen peered over the top to rain fire down upon them. Craven took aim with his pistol and fired, killing one and striking another in the arm, causing the Frenchman to lose his musket. Yet more took their place and fired back. Craven ducked down as one musket ball clipped his jacket sleeve and the other zipped past his ear. The battle raged back and forth, but they could not gain any ground. The enemy fire was relentless, and they could not charge the final distance without disastrous effects. There was little pause in the enemy fire as the French soldiers took turns firing down before retiring to reload out of sight. The enemy had the peak, and there was nothing to be done about it. The Caçadores were already beginning to give ground and retire in good order as they continued to fire.

"We cannot do it," insisted Matthys.

"If they would just press forward, it could be done. Damn it!" Craven cried angrily.

"No, it cannot, Sir, and continuing will only cost us more lives," snapped Paget defiantly.

Powder smoke wafted over them, and the snap of muzzles igniting above continued as they were peppered with musket fire. He trusted the judgement of the two of them more than anyone, and he could see even Ferreira was of the same mind.

The French had beaten them to the top, and the weight of fire was just too much. There was no way to the top now, but he did not need to give the order to retreat. Many were already falling back, seeing the futility of it all, and he had to accept it himself as he gave up their position and began to withdraw. They soon lost sight of the peak which the French held as it was engulfed in a fog of powder smoke. That at least saved them from the onslaught as the enemy could no longer see them either. Many bodies lay scattered on the slope before them, and many more wounded hobbled away or were helped by their comrades.

Craven led them on as a rabble, a little demoralised, but mostly intact. He stopped for a moment and looked back. French soldiers were advancing into many positions to the West stretching from North to South.

"That is quite a show of force," declared Paget.

"Rest here a while and be ready to march," Craven gave the order to Ferreira as he and Paget went on, approaching Wellington. He watched every development like a hawk, waiting to dive upon his target at the first opportunity. Infantry were gathering nearby as though some advance was about to be made.

"A noble effort, Major," he declared as Craven approached.

"But not a successful one," he grumbled in reply.

Wellington said nothing.

"You mean to attack, Sir?"

Craven watched soldiers gathering and looked across to see where they might aim. A mass of French troops was isolated to the North where they advanced onto the heights there. Yet Wellington was deep in conversation with many of his fellow officers, including Beresford. It was clear that whatever intentions Wellington had to advance had been shattered as he passed on orders for the assembled troops to withdraw.

"Back and forth, time and time again," moaned Craven.

"You would have me risk everything without certainty of victory?" Wellington asked.

"Victory is never certain, but it cannot be obtained without an attempt." Craven failed to hide a scowl from the General.

"I am right there with you, Major. For I feel all the same frustrations, but we must not let our temper, nor our passions get a hold of us and make us do things we will regret. You more than anybody should know that."

"I'm afraid that is not a lesson the Major has yet learnt."

Wellington was stunned that Lieutenant Paget would speak up in such a way, and yet Craven seemed to find it amusing. But Wellington kept his eyes on the potential battlefield before him. The French formations continued to move and appear across the landscape.

"They look for a weakness," said Paget.

"Yes, they do, or what they believe is one." Wellington turned to an aide-de-camp and passed on orders which soon saw a British infantry division push forward to protect his front, as if he expected the enemy to march directly on their position. And yet their Commander sighed as he realised no attack was coming, "Will you join me for a modest luncheon?"

"Of course," replied Craven.

Though he knew that meant the potential for a battle had ground to a halt as Wellington and his staff retired to a farmyard nearby. Craven and Paget followed, but the Lieutenant kept looking over his shoulder, hoping and praying the enemy would advance. They could hear sporadic musket fire in the distance as small skirmishes continued, but nothing of great significance.

Wellington sat down to eat some plain chicken that had been laid out for him in the yard atop tables pulled out from the farmhouse. Craven was glad to join him, but Paget would not. He waited twenty yards away, looking out towards the French positions and the roads which any messages might be delivered to them. Wellington sat back and looked most relaxed as he enjoyed his meal. It was not the look of a man on the edge of the most important battle of his life.

"It will not come today, will it?"

"No, it will not," he admitted.

Craven huffed with frustration.

"We will retire to Rodrigo, then? And even perhaps back into Portugal once more?"

"We will secure a more favourable position."

"Then we run from the fight," snarled Craven.

"When you are out there with sword and pistol and rifle, and you can do battle, but you know that you will not win, what do you do?"

"I look for another way."

"And that is what we will do."

"I do not run for the border," protested Craven.

"Major, you command a few dozen men, sometimes a few hundred, but I command many tens of thousands. It is not the same."

"I know," grimaced Craven in acceptance but also with great frustration.

"When the time is right, we will do battle, but not a moment before. We have waited years for this moment, and we will not squander it because we could not wait another day, another week, or even another month."

"Yes, Sir," admitted Craven.

"Marmont is my challenge, what of yours, Colonel Mizon?"

Craven was surprised he would even ask.

"I have not encountered that wretch again, but I will."

"The likelihood is he will be close now I would imagine,

as what we do here will matter more to him than anything."

"Why?"

"You know how important this battle is to everyone, and perhaps because I had Major Thornhill ensure the French knew you would be here."

"Me? Why would you do such a thing?"

"Because Mizon wants you, Major, and he has the ear of many men above him. We want the enemy to come at us. We want them to be impatient, and what better way than to let that Colonel know he has a chance at you here."

"You think an entire army of fifty thousand French soldiers would march to battle just for a chance at me?"

"No, but a man with a little power and influence who wants you that badly might engineer a plan to make it happen," smiled Wellington.

"I think you put too high a value on my head, Sir!"

"Well, Major, the enemy certainly do. I have heard great rewards have been offered for your capture, or death. As much as you are a nightmare for those who command you, you are far worse to the enemy, and they know it. And so do I, or I would not let you go on serving in this army."

"I have a value and so you tolerate me?" Craven smiled back at him.

"Precisely, though I have to tolerate far worse officers with far less value, and so it is not always such a burden as you might imagine."

"Then I must try harder," joked Craven.

Wellington laughed as he sat back and relaxed further, and they all accepted their fate. There would be no battle that day, and therefore no victory nor glory, but also no risk of defeat. It was deeply unsatisfying, but there seemed nothing for it.

"Look at him, how does he never lose an ounce of that enthusiasm?" Wellington gazed out towards Paget, noticing he was like an overly enthusiastic puppy.

"Youth."

"Were you like that when you were younger?"

"No," admitted Craven.

"Indeed, and neither was I. In fact, many people believed I would never make anything of myself at all, and I can understand why, for I was the precise opposite of that fine young man."

"It is most annoying, or it was. I thought it was. But in time I realise we all need a friend like that in life."

"Is that what Mr Paget is to you?" Wellington asked curiously.

"Friend, family, brother, he is all of them."

"He will be as disappointed as you and I; perhaps even more so, but he will not show it."

"I know, he bears a great deal of weight on those small shoulders."

They took their eyes from him for just a brief moment as they relaxed, seemingly expecting the hope to force a battle had passed when Paget's voice echoed out.

"Sir!"

Wellington and Craven shot to their feet in the hope of some news which might change the day. An aide-de-camp raced towards them and soon passed Paget who rushed back to hear for himself.

"The enemy are in motion, My Lord," declared the ADC rather stoically.

Wellington sighed with disappointment.

"Very well," he groaned. He had heard the same news several times throughout the morning only to find it was of little consequence.

"Observe what they are doing," he grumbled afterward.

"I think they are extending their left, My Lord," replied the ADC.

"The devil they are!" Wellington cried in disbelief.

Paget's eyes glistening with excitement.

"Give me my glass. Quickly, man!"

It was handed to him, and he stormed off to a vantage point where he could get a better look with his telescope. A dozen staff followed and Craven and Paget, too. Craven used his own glass and could barely believe what he was seeing. Marmont and several divisions were holding firm on the heights of the Greater Arapile, which was directly Southwest of the corner of Wellington's force. Yet other French columns were now separating and creating huge gaping holes between their formations as they stretched out far West along the Southern edge of Wellington's position. They were in such extended order that they were vulnerable and seemingly moved without any fear of a counterattack, as if they could move without consequence or threat.

"By God!" Wellington cried in delight, "That will do!"

He rushed back to the farmyard and unfolded a map on the table before them. He quickly studied it with much haste and anticipation. Paget was beaming as he knew what this meant. The stagnation was over. The time for action had come.

They all watched Wellington formulate a plan in a matter of just a few moments. A remarkable thing to behold, as he created an entire battle plan singlehandedly based on an evolving situation in such a short space of time.

"We will hit them all at once. We have the high ground, and we are concealed. They do not know our number nor our positions, and now they spread their lines thin. They think us too timid to attack them! Ha!"

"All these weeks waiting and not wanting to take risks, and now we risk everything all at once?" Paget whispered to Craven.

"Indeed, Lieutenant. This was the moment we have been waiting for. The moment the enemy underestimated us and took us for fools. They think they can do as they please without recumbence, and what do you say to that, Mr Paget?" Wellington roared.

"I think it's time we showed them our mettle, Sir!"

"Yes, and we will! We will, indeed!"

He rushed for his horse to gallop off and deliver his orders in person, so he could be sure everyone understood them fully and all knew the part they must play. All except for Craven and the Salford Rifles who he had left to their own devices.

"What will we do, Sir?" Paget asked.

"A great blow will be dealt at the French left, and I should be there to see it, wouldn't you?"

"I would, Sir! I would!"

They rushed back to their small force.

"Ferreira, stay here and assist where you are needed. Everyone else who can ride, you are with me!" Craven cried.

"You mean to join a cavalry charge, don't you?" Timmerman grinned as he pulled himself up into the saddle.

"We have an opportunity here today, but it can only be exploited with speed. We must move like the wind, and so if is cavalry we must be, then that is what we shall be."

"Spoken like a cavalryman. I think you wear the wrong uniform."

"And you, too, and you always have, you damned rogue!"

"James Craven calling me a rogue? An honour!"

CHAPTER 16

Cannons roared in the distance as skirmishes and artillery duels continued, but excitement was building as they galloped on, trying to keep up with Wellington. He darted about the lines for many miles handing out his orders so that there would be no uncertainty nor delay. Two divisions of British infantry with Portuguese in support were marching forward to make an advance on the French left flank.

"They'll never see it coming, will they, Sir?" Paget asked excitedly. The formations were still concealed on the reverse slope and out of sight of the French forces advancing West, without any clue what danger they were falling into. Yet Wellington still pressed on even further to the West, "Where does Sir Arthur go, Sir?"

"He does not mean to just engage the enemy head on, but to roll up their flank and secure such a decisive victory that the enemy cannot recover."

"Yes, yes!"

Paget realised the moment had finally come. The moment they had waited for and struggled to reach for months on end. It felt as the whole of Wellington's army was on the move, yet so little of it could be seen by Marmont's force, and they would not know it until the last moment.

Soon enough they came across the whole of Packenham's Division who had marched from the North, and they rode up just as Wellington had handed out his orders to his brother-in-law. Packenham acknowledged Craven with a friendly smile as he approached. The two had been close ever since he had taken Craven's side in the tragedy of Colonel Bevan, a move that had almost cost them both their careers in the army. A career which Craven had never placed any value in the past, and yet now it was everything to him. Paget could hardly believe what he was seeing. The whole of the Third Division was marching around the enemy's flank under Packenham's command.

The Connought Rangers proudly marched on past them, with many more regiments on the same path, including numerous Caçadores. In the distance they could see a mass of British cavalry advancing in support of Packenham's Division, and Le Marchant was approaching them to hear any news for himself.

"Finally, a chance at 'em ey, Major?" he asked Craven.

"Yes, Sir."

"Would you ride with us?"

"I am no cavalryman."

"We can make one of you this day," smiled Le Marchant.

Craven looked to Paget for his opinion, but the beaming smile told him everything.

"It would be an honour."

Wellington coughed to bring them to silence. "Now, gentlemen, our task here today is not to scare the enemy, nor to provoke them or skirmish with them. I mean to strike with such a blow as Nelson did at Trafalgar, and you men will be the spearhead that punches through the enemy line just like Nelson did."

"I wouldn't mention that around our Spanish allies, Sir," replied Craven, remembering how the fleet Nelson had faced was a combined French and Spanish force. The rest of them laughed at the prospect.

"Where are they?" Wellington laughed, causing more laughter amongst them all. For the Spanish regulars still had a fearful reputation amongst the British and Portuguese army.

"We will see it done," insisted Packenham.

"See that you do. We do not seek a victory in the newspapers here today. I mean to crush Marmont's army." Wellington looked toward the enemy advances to the South, "Do you see those fellows on the hill, Pakenham? Throw your division into columns at them directly and drive them to the devil."

Packenham saluted his brother-in-law and commander.

"Let me shake the hand of a conqueror," he declared boldly.

But Wellington smiled and shook his head, for he would not tempt fate by accepting such an accolade before seeing the victory through. He turned and rode on as Packenham's Division continued to march on.

"Win here today and live to see the end of it, and you will be a Colonel," declared Packenham.

"Why would I want that?" replied Craven sternly.

"Craven, I think you are the only man in this whole army who isn't seeking promotion," laughed Packenham.

Le Marchant and his fellow cavalry officers were discussing things amongst themselves.

"You still want us?" Craven asked.

Le Marchant shrugged as if it was a silly question.

"My men have seen what you can do, and I know what you can do. And you must put that sword to work!" He was looking at the cavalry sword fixed to Craven's saddle, whilst he had his Andrea Ferrara slung about his waist.

"It has seen plenty already."

"Good, then it can see a little more, and when we heroes are finished here with our sabres, we shall ensure the heavies put down their old broadswords and take a step forward into the modern day."

Craven looked past him to the other officers from the heavy cavalry regiments to see the doubt and suspicion on their faces as they clutched onto their long, straight swords with their bulbous ladder type guards. Their swords looked to be twice as cumbersome as the sword Le Marchant had designed, and yet they carried them with pride.

Le Marchant noticed their disapproving glances and laughed as he had clearly failed to convince them many times before.

"You are with me, aren't you, Craven?" he asked as he held up his sheathed sword, the design of which he was so proud of, "Well? You are a champion of my sword, are you not?"

"It is certainly a formidable cutting blade."

"You think you could come up with a better one?" he asked accusingly.

"For the cavalry? No, I will leave it to cavalrymen."

Le Marchant laughed.

"You should go into politics, Major, for you have a great way with words."

"It will be a cold day in hell," he recoiled.

"Then let us be on our way, gentlemen, for we have a battle to win!"

The sound of horses galloping towards them drew their eyes. It was Timmerman rushing to their side as eagerly as Paget would if he was at risk of missing a great event. He rode up to Craven as Le Marchant and the others separated to lead their columns forward.

"I didn't think you'd come. In fact, a few of us even bet on it."

"We all know you're a terrible gambler," replied Timmerman with a straight face.

"That's true, and yet you are here to ride with me."

"If you'll have me," replied Timmerman humbly.

"We could sure use you. All that anger, all that wrath and fury you have felt towards me and others. Let it all out now, today, but on the enemy who are before you, on the French," pleaded Craven.

"I will and, Craven?"

"Yes?"

"My men have spotted Colonel Mizon. He is out there, on the French left where we are driving."

"He is?" Craven asked in amazement and excitement.

"Yes. I will fight here beside you like a lion, but you have to promise me that you will not let him live if you get another shot at him. He is too dangerous. You let Bouchard live once and remember what it cost. He is still out there, plotting against us and doing all sorts of damage. If you get a chance at Mizon, do not miss."

"I had a chance to end you more than once, but I did not," smiled Craven.

"And perhaps that was a mistake, but now it is one you have to live with, too."

"Le Marchant has asked that we ride in support of his cavalry, will you join us?"

"I already have."

They went on to join the cavalry column as Packenham's force advanced in four columns in the natural cover of the land. They made quite the racket as the equipment they all carried from cartridge boxes to sheathed swords and cartridge boxes bashed against their bodies, and hundreds of hooves echoed out over the dry ground. And yet the distant sound of musket and cannon fire would conceal their movements until the very last moment, just as the hills of Salamanca did.

On and on they went, and soon enough they could hear musket fire far closer as the head of Packenham's column had finally encountered the enemy. It was not long before they saw it with their own eyes. Portuguese light cavalry had engaged the French troops who were in a panic, as the cavalry had got in front and behind. The rest of the French soldiers were fleeing in a panic to get up the hill ahead of them where they might find some safety and stage a defence. It was the hill Wellington had told Packenham to assault, and now they were going to get their chance.

They could see the Connaught Rangers who had passed them earlier making an advance at the head of a brigade up the hill. As they did so, the Major commanding them was shot down. Such a scene might have caused many a regiment to run, but the Rangers were only incensed by it and redoubled their efforts. They charged furiously up the hill in such a forceful and determined assault as nobody could stand against it. Canister and grape shot riddled their ranks, but nothing would stop them. The French infantry atop the peak were in a loose rabble, as if not at all feeling they were in danger. But no amount of musket fire would stop the Connaught Rangers and those who charged beside them. Musket volleys soon gave way to the clang of cold steel as sword and bayonet met, but the French soldiers there were quickly reduced to state of panic-stricken poor fools. They were scattered from the hilltop and fled for their lives. The British and Irish soldiers pursued them and charged on to see them off, vanishing from view to those below.

"It's happening. It's really happening!" Paget cried.

It was too soon to be celebrating a victory, but they could all feel triumph in the air. They could smell it, and they could feel it. It had been such a long road to this point, and it felt as though nothing could hold them back as the British and Portuguese light dragoons stormed on to support the infantry who were smashing the French left flank. Powder smoke wafted across the great long battlefield. They could hear cannon fire and musket volleys to the East.

The general advance had begun, just as Wellington had planned it and intended for it to proceed. No longer would this be some small skirmish or back and forth. The time a stand-up fight between the two great armies had come, and nothing could stop the great clash. They rode on and soon came over the ridge to find a scene of chaos. The ground was scattered with the dead and wounded, mostly French soldiers. Much of the dry ground was on fire. The blazing gorse let off a great intensity of heat and huge clouds of smoke far denser and more intoxicating than the sulphur filled pale clouds of powder smoke, which was already choking them all and burning their eyes.

"There they are my lads! Just let them feel the temper of your bayonets!" Pakenham called out.

Packenham's infantry had smashed the French flank, but they had now marched directly into an unbroken French brigade who held firm, and to make matters worse French cavalry were threatening their flank. Not only could they stop the advance, but they could also do horrific damage to the isolated infantry. Packenham rode back and forth amongst his soldiers, crying out for his battalions to form square. Many of his subordinates did likewise, but the infantry was in disorder of the chaotic advance. They were engulfed in smoke from the fires all around them, and so discipline could not be maintained, and orders were not enacted. The French cavalry were about to launch their attack, and the French infantry looked on with glee at the chance of launching an assault with bayonet and sword to assist their cavalrymen in what could be a slaughter.

But the French cavalry had not seen the British and Portuguese light cavalry advancing on them, and they darted forward, sweeping the surprised cavalry before them.

Craven looked at his pocket watch. The battle had raged for merely a single hour and a smile came to his face.

"What is it, Sir?" Paget asked.

"One hour, and two French Divisions have been smashed. Two whole divisions killed, wounded, or captured, and a third in not much better a state."

It was like a dream. They had all felt and worried that a battle would never come, and now they were riding on to such a great victory that few dared dream of.

Le Marchant's British heavies continued their advance on Pakenham's left flank, and as they closed in, they drew ever closer to the fighting at the centre of the battle near the village of Los Arapiles. The British heavies were great big men on the largest horses. They wielded their massive brutish swords, which they whipped around as if they were merely singlesticks, but with a devastating effect on all they made contact with. They were a powerful and brutish instrument like the mounted knights of old, who would smash almost any target they charged upon en masse. But they were also well known for being rash and ill-disciplined, being in the wrong place at the wrong time.

That was not the case now, not under the supervision of Wellington, Packenham, and Le Marchant, and they were most eager to take their part in the battle. The fog of war from the burning ground and powder smoke began to lift a little as the heavies made their advance. They could see French infantry forming up in square to receive them, and they were right to do so. Nothing but a well-formed square would hinder the advance of the battering ram that the heavies were renowned for.

Yet it was not the British heavies who were of most immediate concern to the French. British infantry advanced up from a concealed undulation and formed up to pour volley after volley into the square, a most bizarre scene, and a most unfortunate one for the French. The square was strong at withstanding cavalry, but it could send out a fraction of the fire towards the lines of British infantry who now poured down fire into them, weakening them further as Le Marchant's menacing force went forward. The thunderous roar of the hundreds of British heavies soon captured their attention as they soared forward diagonally to strike the flank of the crumbling square.

"I told you, Craven, today we will make a cavalryman of you!" Le Marchant drew out his sabre.

There was a great excitement as they passed through the British infantry who cheered on the cavalry. They stormed forward and crashed into the French line before they could reform square. The British heavies crashed into the enemy with an immense velocity, and the impact was enough to cause many to run immediately. The great big broadswords of the troopers lashed down against any who were bold and brave enough to stand, but in a few brief moments, the French line was smashed and in full retreat. The British infantry advanced quickly amongst them to seize prisoners. Le Marchant swung his sabre about his head as he rallied many to his side, including Craven who was yet to use his sword for anything. The first charge had been such a quick success, he had been left idle. Ahead of them they could see another French infantry regiment of the Line preparing to defend against cavalry.

"We do not stop here!" Le Marchant galloped on to lead a charge at the second line of French soldiers.

No order needed to be given. Everyone knew what had to be done. Craven and his closest friends charged on after Le Marchant's heavies, struggling to keep up as now they had been released there was no stopping them. A volley erupted from the French line ahead, and several of the red-coated cavalrymen were knocked from their horses, but it was not nearly enough to stop them. They ploughed into the French lines just as ferociously as they had the previous line. Sabres and broadswords hacked back and forth as they came amongst the enemy who had caused them so much trouble for months and years on end. Frustrations were taken out.

Craven finally found a use for his sabre as he hacked down at one sergeant and cleaved through his hat. A bayonetted musket came for him from another Frenchman, but he reacted by hacking down at it with the sabre Le Marchant had gifted him. The heavy blade and the arm wielding it caused the musket to be launched from the Frenchman's hands, leaving him with nothing. He turned and quickly fled.

Craven stopped for a moment to peer around at what was going on all around him. It was a total rout as there was no formation left to the French infantry. It was every man for himself for those who remained to try and fight in a futile attempt. All around him his closest friends battled with swords in hand. Paget, Matthys, Vicenta, Birback, Caffy, Amyn, Moxy, Ellis, and even Timmerman, who he now counted amongst his friends, were hacking the enemy down. Those who surrendered and laid down their weapons were given mercy, but any who continued to fight were shown none.

It had cost them all a great deal to get to this point, and the memories of Ciudad Rodrigo, Badajoz, and the forts of Salamanca were still very raw. It was time to get some payback. Paget hacked and stabbed back and forth, killing three by himself in just a few strokes, but the action was short-lived, as those who could flee did, whilst most were taken prisoner. A second French line had been smashed, and they had lost twice as many as prisoners as they had to musket fire and sabre. They were losses the enemy could not afford as the two armies were of near equal size when the contest had finally begun.

Cries of ecstasy rang out from infantry and cavalry alike. It was already a great triumph, and yet they could see to the East that many more battles raged all along the line.

"Craven!"

He looked out to see a line of French light cavalry forming on their flank, though they appeared hesitant to advance on the great force of British heavies and the infantry all around them. Yet Craven quickly realised it was not the force of several hundred light cavalry he was being alerted to, but an officer who was amongst them. Colonel Mizon, glaring at him furiously.

"That is him?" Le Marchant rode up beside Craven.

"Yes, the bastard who must die."

"Then kill him," insisted Le Marchant.

But Craven looked hesitant as another French infantry line lay ahead, and they looked stronger and more prepared than the previous two. Le Marchant smiled.

"We can manage this quite fine. Go after him. Now!"

"That is the sword, the sword I promised you."

"Then get it for me."

Le Marchant cried out as he waved his sword about and led the heavies on to their third assault on a French line. At this rate it seemed like nothing would stop them as the French positions rolled up one after another. Craven looked to his own small force, and then back to Mizon's, who outnumbered them by four or five to one.

"Do it," grinned Timmerman.

Yet he did not want to sacrifice them all for his own vengeance. But the gallop of horses at their side drew his attention to a force of fresh British and Portuguese light cavalry who came storming into view and raced on at Mizon's force.

"Yes!" Craven dug his heels in and stormed on to join them in their charge.

They raced on beside the light cavalry, which caused quite a look of concern as Mizon turned and fled. Craven drew to a halt on a ridge to get a better view and looked back to Le Marchant's heavies. They smashed into their third infantry line like a battering ram. It seemed like nothing could stop them. Pakenham's infantry division was reforming to continue their advance relentlessly as they circled around the French left flank. There was nothing to stop them now, and even though battles raged all along the line between the two armies, the great right hook had smashed the flank of Marmont's army.

"We lost him again," bristled Paget.

But Craven looked about to see the whole of the right flank of Wellington's army advancing in with a menacing approach. The battle lines had changed significantly. Both armies were in perfect parallel and reached from North to South, but of most concern was the centre where a bloody battle still raged. British and Portuguese forces now withdrew from a massive assault from the Greater Arapile to the Lesser Arapile, which was not only the centre of the Anglo Portuguese army, but had also been Wellington's staging post throughout.

"This isn't over. Mizon's time will come." Craven looked to the triumphant charge of Le Marchant's heavies. They had utterly smashed the French flank and caused them to flee at great speed. It was an achievement rarely seen by any soldier, even one who had spent years fighting in this war.

"Sir! Look!" Paget cried.

His attention was drawn to the centre of the battlefield where the French pressed hard against the Lesser Arapile, and where the British and Portuguese forces had launched their attack against the Greater one and failed. But it was not the French advance Paget was pointing to, but to a mass of infantry marching to oppose them, of which on the closest flank to them was the main force of the Salford Rifles under the command of Ferreira.

"Sir, if they take the centre, if they take the Lesser Arapile, all our advantage could be lost. All hope of a great victory might be lost, and worse!"

Craven looked for a moment towards Mizon as he fled into the distance. He was so close and almost in reach, and yet felt so far.

"Sir, will we leave our brothers to withstand the charge?"

Paget could see Craven contemplating which road to take.

CHAPTER 17

"Finally, a chance at the enemy, if only Craven were here," said Quental as they advanced towards the greater French force who had forced the British infantry in the centre to flee.

"You think he wouldn't have been in the thick of it?" replied Ferreira nervously. He looked back at the soldiers of the Salford Rifles marching on confidently under his command, but not without fear. And worst of all, they were missing so many of their comrades who they would much like to have by their side when they closed with the enemy.

Light cavalry from both sides swirled all about as they engaged one another, and great masses of infantry descended upon one another. It was the moment that would make or break the battle for both sides, and everyone knew it. British and Portuguese infantry poured into centre of the line to resist the French advance, a mix of several different divisions. Ferreira was just four hundred yards from the enemy infantry, but they were not in loose formation and skirmishing, but advancing as a block to act as line infantry; a role they were not at all suited to with the slow reloading times of their rifles. But skirmishing did not matter here. They had to force back the French advance with weight of fire, and everyone knew it.

"It's the Major!" Nooth shouted.

A roar of jubilant celebration rang out as Craven's mounted force approached to reunite the Salford Rifles as one. The mounted element took up a position on the right flank to skirt the riflemen and protect them from any stray enemy cavalry.

"I was worried you'd miss it!" Ferreira cried as Craven approached.

"Not a chance."

"Will you assume command?"

Craven looked to another Portuguese battalion approaching and could see them watching and seeing all.

"It's yours, Captain, now get up that hill!"

Craven pointed toward the Greater Arapile where the French had made their advance with cannons still roaring from that elevated position. Ferreira saluted as Craven took up his position on the flank. Moxy and many of the others had pressed on forward and were taking well aimed shots from the saddle, which was no easy feat. Though the mass of French infantry was no small target.

There was no cover to be had on the open ground between the two elevated positions from which the two armies had contested. The ground was still burning in many locations, and artillery fire from the French-held Arapile continued to rain down upon them. But on they went as a great many lines of

British and Portuguese infantry came together in a great formation and came into range with the enemy. The first British volley rang out in near perfect symphony and wobbled the French troops had that had formed up to face them.

A great duel was about to begin, as if a fleet of warships had come alongside one another to exchange broadsides. And yet it took a little while for the French to regain order. The almost majestic long British and Portuguese line was already loaded and ready to fire a second before they had loosed their first. The effects were devastating. The field became a fog of powder smoke and fresh fires were ignited by burning cartridge wadding.

The French fired into this fog, and so began an exchange of volleys, though the fate of the enemy had been decided in the first few, and a waft of fresh air carried away much of the powder smoke. The enemy looked beleaguered and ready to run.

"Prepare to Charge!"

Nobody could tell where the order had originated from, but it was echoed by many officers down the line until it reached Ferreira who roared the command out loud. Every soldier, except those mounted, had their bayonets or sword bayonets affixed already, as was necessary to protect against any surprise attack or sudden arrival of cavalry.

"Advance!"

They began the march forward, and whilst the enemy continued to fire at them, it was sporadic and would not stop them.

"Charge!"

They rushed on across the open plains as British and Portuguese troops stormed both the Greater and Lesser Arapile, and few Frenchmen stayed to oppose them. The French counterattack of the centre was not only halted, but it was also broken, as Ferreira led a rush onto the Greater Arapile. They found the French had abandoned the guns they had used to fire down from that position all day. Most of the French divisions were rushing towards the cover of the forests to the South, though many fought as they retired, and one whole division remained as an obstacle before Wellington's army. One last barrier that would stop the rest of the French army from being swept up and killed or captured.

Nine infantry battalions had been formed in thin lines on a hill to the East, and a further battalion formed in square protected each of their flanks. It looked like a fortress from a distance, but worse than that, they were formed in thin lines, which would maximise their firepower against anyone who tried to oppose them. And yet a great many British troops pressed on to try and drive them from their position to seal a complete and total victory. For the sun was going down, and light was already beginning to fail.

Craven could hardly believe it. For the first part of the battle in the afternoon seemed just a few moments before. They had battled for several hours as they made their way Eastward. The British infantry hurried on to make their attack before those on the flanks were even reformed and ready for it. Time was against them now.

The French were well formed on a craggy ridge at such an angle as they could fire down in multiple ranks. Those making the assault would have to struggle to make the climb under immense fire. Grape shot smashed the British lines, and as they reached within a hundred yards, a tremendous fire erupted from the French musketry.

To those watching on from afar it looked as if the entire hill was a sheet of fire. Musket and cannon fire lit up the position in the failing light, and fires continued to rage amongst the two sides. At one hundred yards both gave fire. Volley after volley was exchanged, inflicting the most horrific casualties on both sides. The quick victory the attacking force had hoped to achieve was lost.

Finally, both sides were shattered, but the pressing advance of the rest of Wellington's army was too much for the rear guard. They began to scatter and flee for the forests where the rest of the army had run to seek shelter. And yet they were pursued all of the way as Craven led his force to sweep them away. The Salford Rifles had become scattered as they pressed on as a loose skirmishing force, for even in retreat, many of the French soldiers would not lay down their weapons nor flee outright.

Many of the enemy were covered in blood, with ripped uniforms and shrouded in dirt and powder burns, and fight on they did. Powder smoke wafted by. The battle had reduced to a running skirmish along a broad front, as Wellington's army pressed on to inflict as much damage as it could before the day was done.

Craven galloped past one Frenchman and hacked down onto his head. He raised his sabre to another to notice he was but a boy, not more than fifteen-years-old, and he stayed his hand, letting the lad run. But in the moment, he stayed his hand and showed mercy, a pistol shot struck his arm. He winced with pain and looked forward. Colonel Mizon was holding a pistol with smoke rising from the barrel from the shot he had fired.

Craven quickly checked his wound to see the small ball was lodged in the top of his arm, but it was buried in the very edge of his flesh and barely impeded his movement, in spite of it being his right arm of which he was most skilled. The ball would have to be pulled out later, but it was merely lodged in the soft tissue, and he shrugged it off.

"You missed!" Craven roared.

"Hardly!" Mizon snarled back at him.

Mizon looked ragged from the battle, but he seemed determined to draw one last small victory from the horrific defeat that day, and that victory would be to claim Craven's life. Craven was happy to oblige and give him a chance at it.

"Let us finish this, you and I!"

Craven looked to the sabre in his hands, the one Le Marchant had given him, and back to the beautiful silver hilted spadroon which Mizon carried. It was the very opposite situation to which he would want to find himself in, and he looked down at his beloved Andrea Ferrara blade still dangling by his side. For a moment he considered drawing it to make for a fair fight, as it was the far more agile sword, and in a duel the sword that could move fastest was so often of great advantage.

But then Craven noticed the purse Le Marchant had given him to purchase a sword for him, and the memory made him look upon the cavalry sabre fondly. He had promised to win a great sword for the cavalry officer, and he would honour him by doing it with the sabre he had gifted him. The same sword he himself had designed and poured all of his years of experience and knowledge as a cavalryman into. He was determined to win with the sword he had been gifted, and nothing would stop him. He held it up before him and made his charge. Mizon did likewise as the two closed at one another as if they were jousting.

Mizon attempted to plunge his sword into Craven's chest, but Craven parried it away and tried to cut around. Mizon's lighter and faster sword whipped around and slashed across his chest, opening a long but shallow cut across his uniform and body. Craven winced a little again, but it was a superficial wound that he shrugged off even though he knew Matthys would be most upset. The Sergeant would be the one stitching up both his wounds and his uniform. Craven smirked at the thought of it as he looked up at the brutishly broad sabre tip of the blade in his hands and remembered how Le Marchant had used it against him.

They charged at one another again, but this time both blades glanced from one another with no hits inflicted. So, they rode in against one another again but at a steadier pace so that they might battle it out without another pass. They were equally eager and frustrated. Craven struck first with a feint, deceiving Mizon on one side before cutting around to the other, but his blade was not near fast enough to outsmart Mizon with his lightning quick blade. The Frenchman made it to the parry comfortably as he egged his horse on and tried to cut around at the back of Craven's neck as he went past.

With the lift of his sword guard, and a drop of the point of his blade over his right shoulder, Craven parried the blow out of the corner of his eye and behind him. They wheeled back around and stared at one another from ten yards as chaos ensued all around them. The last of the French infantry battled it out in a raged fighting retreat through the woods. Sporadic musket and rifle fire rang out and cold steel met. Paget caught a glimpse of Craven and Mizon. He paused for a moment and gasped as if he wanted to go in and help.

"Leave them be," growled Matthys.

He did not need to explain why, and Paget was well aware. This was personal.

"There!" Matthys cried out as a Frenchman cried out angrily, charging Paget with a musket, the bayonet fixed.

Paget pulled Augustus' reins to bring him around so that he was safely out of the way, and Paget put himself in harm's way to protect his best friend. He cut down against the bayonet and locked his sword into the elbow of it before reaching across and grabbing hold of the muzzle with his bridle hand. The infantryman was undone and completely at Paget's mercy as he presented the point of his sword to the fellow's chest. The man was of a similar size and age to Paget, though he looked to be in a horrible state. His uniform was in tatters, and he was burnt, cut, and shot through, and yet he now also looked distraught. He let go of his weapon and made no further resistance.

"Go on," whispered Paget as he threw the musket down to the ground.

The anger and aggression in the man's eyes quickly faded away before he realised the dangers still remaining all around him as the battle continued. He turned and fled as quickly as his exhausted legs would carry him. But Charlie rode up beside him in disgust.

"A man tries to kill you and you let him live!"

"I do, and I will do it again. I didn't come here to Portugal and Spain to kill. I never wanted to kill anyone, and I will only do it if I must. I think you were the same once," he replied unapologetically.

She could not disagree, and her recent realisations that she no longer lived to fulfil a bloodlust and revenge came flooding back to her.

"Yes, but don't let your honour get you killed. Craven made that mistake with Bouchard."

"He did not spare Bouchard for honour, but selfishness and the pursuit of his own glory," snapped Paget as they watched the final remnants of the French army vanish into the woodland ahead.

"And now?" Charlie directed his gaze to the epic mounted duel still raging between Craven and Mizon, which many of those around them had gathered to behold.

It was an exceptional display of skill. Craven used every lesson Le Marchant had taught him about mounted combat, but Mizon's masterful crafted blade was lightning fast and causing the Major all sorts of problems. He struggled to find openings and barely made it to some parries. Back and forth they went, blow after blow with little achieved until Mizon managed to flick a cut against Craven's left cheek. It was a light blow but enough to open a blood wound. Craven was reminded more of Le Marchant's lessons and parried a quick cut to the left of his face with the spine of his own sabre. He used the motion to wrench Mizon's blade aside and whirl into a strong horizontal cut, and yet it was stopped by a quick parry.

Craven was in no mood to be trifled with now. He was not there to play a game or prove a point. He wanted his opponent dead, and he knew he must now fight just as Le Marchant did, with ruthless power. He was done using the cunning of his own sword skills and instead took a page from Le Marchant's book. He closed in with Mizon and rained down several brutal vertical blows, causing Mizon to lift into a hanging position to take the heavy percussive blows.

Mizon was smiling back at him, safe in the knowledge that no strike was getting through, but Craven had not intended for them to do so. He was lulling Mizon into a false sense of security. Finally, Craven lifted up his brutal sabre and exaggerated the move as if to power another vertical cut with double the strength of the previous ones. The motion caused Mizon to lift his own sword to parry it with a hanging position once more. The Frenchman was so confident in his defence just as before, but Craven turned the blade a little to the right and lashed it down with all his force. It avoided the strongest part of his opponent's blade and struck at the centre of Mizon's sword, causing his entire defence to give way as Craven battered through. The sabre blade cleaved into Mizon's collar, and he cried out in pain as he looked at the wound in disbelief, knowing he was finished.

"Bouchard will avenge me. He will find you, and he will kill you."

"Let him come."

Craven ripped the sabre from the Frenchman's body and thrust the broad tip into his chest to finish him for good. He retrieved the blade and watched as Mizon fell dead from his saddle. Craven breathed a sigh of relief as he leapt from his horse and picked up the sword of his enemy, which he had coveted from the moment he had first set eyes upon it. Paget rode up before him.

"It is done, Sir!"

"What is done?"

"The victory we needed! It is ours!"

He looked around to see the last remnants of the French

army scattered and fleeing from sight as the sun finally set. Everyone was exhausted. There was not a soldier nor a horse in the army who was not entirely spent, but it was now only dawning on Craven what had been achieved. He had been so fixated on their tiny bit of the battlefield that he was only now realising what an immense triumph it had been. Cheers and cries of relief and joy rang out from the exhausted army for as far as they could see and hear. It was the moment they had all been working for. It was the moment they had been looking for ever since Talavera three years back.

Craven took a knee so that he might rest for a moment, for it seemed as though they had achieved the unimaginable. That morning they had thought all hope of doing battle was lost. They thought they would once again be retreating into Portugal in the fate they seemed doomed to repeat.

The day was over, and the army was spent, but it had been a total and complete victory, the likes of which few had ever seen or envisaged. The Salford Rifles began to gather loosely together, having suffered remarkably few casualties, having not borne the brunt of the horrific fire exchanged in the bloody musket duels.

"Gentlemen!"

Timmerman untied a brace of six canteens from his saddle and passed them around. One he tossed to Craven who was glad of some refreshment, and yet he took a sip to find it was not water, but wine. He almost spat it out in surprise but managed to hold it in, not wanting to waste any. The rest of the men soon realised as they cheered Timmerman. They passed the canteens about as they sat down and rested where they had finished fighting. There was no energy for going on. For half an hour they rested until a rider approached at quite some speed, though none of them recognised the young officer.

"Major Craven, Sir, Lord Wellington sends for you."

CHAPTER 18

It was a sombre scene as Craven followed the messenger on with Paget and Ferreira by his side. Exhaustion and fatigue had long set in, and in spite of the remarkable victory, there were still many thousands of dead and wounded for the victor's army. Yet as they approached a party of officers, they could see they were gathering about a single body.

"It's Le Marchant, Sir," Paget declared in horror.

Wellington and many of his generals were gathered around, several of which were wounded themselves from the bloody day.

"Craven, I know you had become close with Gaspard," declared Wellington.

"What happened? Last I saw he was leading a most triumphant charge, the third of the day."

"It was his last. He was shot from the saddle in that very instance and died of his wounds soon after," added Spring.

It was as much a shock to Craven as it was any of them, including Wellington. He looked at the lifeless body of the man who had been so kind to him, and then down to the sheathed trophy sword he had won for the man, the sword he had now come to deliver.

"Was it worth it, Sir?" Craven asked Wellington.

"Nothing is worth the loss of so many good men, but if you are asking after whether we were successful, then yes, more so than we could ever have hoped for."

"Then it was worth it," declared Paget boldly.

Craven wasn't so comfortable with the prospect, but he could see the reasoning in Paget's eyes, and did not need to question his motives.

"And the sword?" Major Spring asked.

"A gift, courtesy of Colonel Mizon."

They all knew what that meant, for there was no chance Craven would have let him live. They watched solemnly as a work party dug a grave for Le Marchant so he might be buried on the battlefield where he had fallen. A great many of the General's cavalry and fellow officers were gathered nearby to see him off in a most modest ceremony.

"Hardly a fitting end for such an officer," declared Paget.

"And yet precisely what he would have wanted. Le Marchant was a practical man. A fighting man. Tomorrow we will press the enemy further, and Le Marchant would want nothing else," insisted Wellington.

"He was a fine gentleman and officer," declared Von Bock, the cavalry officer Craven had seen in action but never been introduced to. The Hanoverian reached out a hand to Craven.

"I saw you ride with General Le Marchant, and I would shake the hand of that man."

Craven accepted.

"That sword, you say it was for him?"

"Yes, and he shall be its last owner."

They watched as Le Marchant's body was lowered into the grave in a blanket, for there was no coffin. It was a hasty battlefield burial. Craven paced over and knelt down beside the open grave. He held out the sword which he had so coveted and promised to the fallen General. He would never have imagined the day he would count such a high-status officer and gentleman amongst his friends. And yet he wished they'd had more time together. For Le Marchant had only served in the Peninsula for a matter of months, compared to the years it had been for many of them. Paget paced over and knelt down beside him.

"This man worked his whole life towards this day, to do what he did. So many years of hard work and strife, all for this moment," declared Paget.

"And it cost him his life."

"But it was a good death. For a man might die for nothing, of sickness or ailment. He might drown or be stabbed in the back. What better death for a great cavalryman than to end it all in the greatest moment of his life. We should all be so lucky."

"Dying is not lucky."

"We all die, Sir, not one of us can escape death."

"No, in that you are right," admitted Craven.

"The General has done all that a man could ever hope to do, and now it is with us and how we honour him."

Craven nodded in agreement. He laid the sword he had taken from Mizon down onto the body of Le Marchant so that they may be united forever. A sentiment which many watching on appreciated, even if they did not understand the whole story behind it. For the gift of a sword from one swordsman to another who had fallen was a great symbolic gesture that they could all support, and none more so in the case of Le Marchant and Craven. Two men who had dedicated their lives to the sword. All were gathered around for the modest ceremony conducted by a military Chaplain. Craven barely heard a word that was spoken as his mind wandered and he remembered Le Marchant. He had so looked forward to seeing the look on his face when he delivered the sword he had spoken so highly of.

Finally, the ceremony came to a close with all looking exhausted. Many soldiers were already asleep where they had ended the day's battle and all but collapsed on their feet. It was not just dusk and the forest that had stopped the chase, but the exhaustion felt by all. All began to part with the loss of Le Marchant on their minds, as it was really a symbol of all they had lost that day.

"I own you now," whispered a voice.

Craven thought he had imagined it but turned about. Colonel Blakeney was gazing upon him with a little glee in his eyes.

"There is no one to protect you now," he seethed.

He was enjoying every second of it as he saw the despair in Craven's eyes, knowing that Le Marchant could not protect him any longer after having come between them and their dispute several times. Paget reached for his sword as if to intervene directly in disgust, but Craven put a hand to his chest to make him stop.

Blakeney smirked further, reminding Craven of the

darkest days of his feud with Timmerman when he was at his very worst. But Blakeney had made a massive miscalculation. He had pushed Craven too far at a time when he was not to be trifled with and would react without care for the consequences, for he no longer cared for whatever they would be.

"You insult me, and you insult the memory of a fine officer and a gentleman!"

"You will address me as your superior," snarled Blakeney as he noticed several other officers watching the scene unfold.

"I will address you with the respect you deserve, which is none. For you have no honour, and I demand satisfaction!"

Blakeney scoffed as he looked around at those beside them. He looked to Wellington to intervene, but the expression his Lordship gave was as bleak and accusing as Craven's. For he had heard every word.

"Will you let an officer of your army address another in such a way, Lord Wellington?"

Wellington merely sighed in disgust and walked away, being unwilling to intervene in light of the Colonel's words and actions, but many more officers and several of Le Marchant's closest friends waited to see the feud unfold.

"Well, Sir, will you apologize?" Bock demanded.

Blakeney hesitated.

"There are no words which would be adequate," cursed Craven.

"Well, then, Colonel Blakeney, do you accept this challenge, or do you forgo your honour?" Bock asked.

Blakeney was in disbelief, but there were too many witnesses for him to shy away.

"I…I accept, but I will not fight this savage with a sword.

We will fight like English gentlemen, with pistols."

"So be it, at first light, and not a moment after. For tomorrow we give chase to the French."

"Yes, quite."

"We meet here, and if you do not come, I will ensure Wellington knows it, and that the whole of England knows it," replied Craven sternly.

"First light, then, and the world shall see who the better man is!" Blakeney then stormed away.

"Do you need a second?" Bock asked.

"I appreciate it, but no."

"General Le Marchant meant a great deal to us all. When you get your chance, do not miss that vile creature."

Craven smiled in appreciation as he left to be with his comrades.

"A duel, with pistols? Are you mad, Sir?" Paget waited until they were out of earshot of the others.

"I have had quite enough of that man. We will see it to an end."

"I think the Lieutenant is more concerned about your marksmanship," replied Ferreira.

Paget would not say it, but he nodded in agreement.

"Whatever must be done, I will do it," replied Craven confidently.

They were soon back with their comrades. They had retired to the ruins of an old farmhouse with several outbuildings, which would provide more comfort overnight than many they had spent beneath the stars. They still passed canteens of wine about, many more than the handful Timmerman had distributed upon their victory that evening.

Paget looked most uncomfortable at the scene.

"Would it please you to know I paid the owner handsomely for this?" Timmerman declared, defending his actions.

"Truly?" Paget asked in surprise.

"You have my word."

"That is worth more to some men than others," growled Craven angrily.

It was clear now that something was wrong, for Craven was furious.

"What is it?" Vicenta asked.

"General Le Marchant is dead, and the Major has challenged Colonel Blakeney to a duel at first light because of offences he caused in light of said events."

A groan of agreement rang out and that shocked nobody. For none of them knew or had such a fondness of Le Marchant as Craven did, and to know he was to fight a duel was the least surprising thing they had heard in weeks.

"The duel is to be fought with pistols," declared Paget.

A gasp of surprise echoed out.

"Fancied a challenge, did you?" Timmerman joked.

But Craven did not see the funny side and remained deadly serious.

"I will meet Colonel Blakeney at first light, and we shall see this settled, but there is something far more important to all of us. Tomorrow morning, we resume the pursuit of Marmont's army. Get your fill of that wine, but not too much. Get some rest. You will need it."

It didn't need to be said. The fatigue caught up on them all soon enough as they made what beds they could in the old ruins. For a few moments Craven was wide awake, deep in thought about the duel the next morning, but his eyes soon drooped, and he fell into a deep sleep. Although he awoke early, just as the first rays of light were hitting the horizon. He got up and walked out from the old house that had been their billets for the night to find the bodies of two British soldiers outside the door, and Timmerman sitting casually against a wall opposite.

"What is this?"

"That would be the two men sent to kill you for a bag of coins each."

Timmerman calmly as he dangled two coin purses as he got up and handed them to Craven.

"Two men came to kill me while I slept?"

"Yes."

"And you were the one to stop them?"

Timmerman shrugged.

"What days we live in," smiled Craven as he thought of the irony of his murderous old adversary having saved his life.

"You should not delay and give Blakeney an excuse to consider you a forfeit."

Paget and Ferreira stepped out from the same house Craven had and looked at the bodies for a moment, shrugging them off as if they did not want to know what had happened.

"Be ready to march. No matter what happens this morning, the Salford Rifles will march, do you understand?" he demanded of Ferreira.

"I do, but, Craven?"

"Yes?"

"Remember you might have something worth dying for,

but you have a great many more reasons to live."

Matthys came out to join them, too. Craven shook his head as he knew his old friend would have something to say to him.

"You would stop me?"

"I wouldn't waste my time trying even if I wanted to. If this must be done, then do it well, and let us be on."

"Get these two in the ground," declared Matthys of the two bodies, without enquiring further about them, for he suspected he knew the story.

Craven went on with just Paget and Timmerman by his side. They were taking the place of his seconds, though he had not asked them to be. It was a vitally important role in the conduct of a duel if it was to be considered at all lawful and honourable. More than anything, the job of a second was to attempt to reconcile the two parties and ensure no blood was spilt, but neither of them was interested in that.

Even Paget wanted to see Blakeney dealt with, even if that meant his death, but he was also concerned. He knew that with a pistol Craven would be able to humble the despicable Colonel without risking his own life, or even his opponent's if he so wished. But a pistol duel was a far greater risk and also a greater gamble, and Paget didn't much like seeing Craven's fate in the hands of a gamble. For he had a fearful reputation as an awful and unlucky gambler.

They marched on to the spot as agreed half-expecting Blakeney to not show up, and yet he was already there waiting for them. Major Spring was there, too, carrying a wooden box under his arm. Wellington was nowhere to be seen, but neither did he condemn nor make any attempt to halt the proceedings.

"Gentlemen, does any man of either party have anything to say?"

There was a bitter silence as nobody wanted to back down now, and Blakeney had a sly grin about him as if he knew something Craven didn't. A camp table was carried up to Spring where he set down the box and opened it.

"You will use these weapons, and they will be loaded here in my presence for all to witness."

Paget looked to Blakeney and his associates, wondering if they would be disappointed or protest somehow, but nothing was said, and yet Major Rooke watched on with glee. The seconds began to load the weapons with everything they needed supplied from the box Major Spring had supplied.

Paget went about loading the pistol for Craven, whilst Timmerman kept a keen eye on Blakeney's men to ensure no tricks were played. Paget did not rush the load as he might in battle. He primed the pan with a flask carrying fine grain powder before taking out a cartridge which he bit off and began to pour down the muzzle. He was sure to tap out every last grain of black powder to ensure none was left wasted in the wadding, which the cartridge became once it was emptied. He took out the ramrod and compressed the cartridge down compactly against the powder, once again ensuring he did as precise a job as possible to try and ensure Craven would have the best performing pistol which could be achieved. In truth, he did not know if it would make a difference, but he wanted to leave as little to chance as possible.

Paget was more scared for Craven now than ever. He hated his fate being left to what was seemingly luck more than anything else. The pistols were passed to the two duellists who stepped up face to face with one another, glaring into each other's eyes with disgust. They turned back-to-back as everyone took up their positions.

"Gentlemen, you will take ten paces forward!" Spring ordered.

"You're a dead man, Craven. I could put a hole through you at fifty paces," whispered Blakeney.

Craven said nothing as he was entirely focused on the task at hand. They both took their steps forward.

"Turn and make ready!"

Both men brought their pistols up near their faces and brought the locks to full cock ready to fire. Paget could barely breathe. It was such a tense moment, and he had a great deal of concern for Craven's safety, but Timmerman was smiling throughout as he was enjoying every moment.

"Present!"

Both men lowered their pistols and took aim at full arm's length extension.

"You may fire when ready."

"I knew you…" began Blakeney.

But Craven did not hesitate, as his quick reactions and his bitter hatred of the Colonel caused him to squeeze the trigger. The fine powder in his pan ignited quickly and caused the main charge to erupt before Colonel Blakeney could even pull the trigger. The lead ball from Craven's pistol struck his adversary in the head between the eyes, and he was dead before his body even began to topple, which it soon did as the Colonel's body crumpled to the ground. It was an abrupt and sudden end to the affair. For many a pistol duel went several rounds, with seconds intervening to find a solution between every shot, many missing or causing superficial damage. But Craven had struck as definitively as a sword thrust through the heart, and Blakeney had not even discharged a single shot.

"Let's get on with this damn war, shall we?" Spring asked with a sigh of relief.

Major Rooke was pale in horror and left quickly as if expecting Craven to come after him like some vengeful spirit, but Craven had no care for him. He tossed his empty pistol at Spring's feet and walked away, leaving Paget stunned before he found his feet to try and catch up.

"Sir, Sir, how did you…"

"Hit my target?"

"Well…yes, Sir."

"I aimed at the middle of my target and pulled the trigger quicker than he did."

"Truly?" Timmerman asked.

"Yes," replied Craven honestly.

Timmerman began to laugh deep down in his stomach so that his whole body was shaking. But Craven did not see the funny side.

"We have wasted enough time on fools like that."

"You are a cold bastard, Craven, and I love you for it," smiled Timmerman.

"Craven?"

They all recognised the boom of Wellington's roar and stopped to face him.

"Yes, Sir?" Craven replied.

"Ugly business it is, a duel between two of my officers."

"Yes, Sir."

"And so it did not happen. Colonel Blakeney died with

honour upon the battlefield of Salamanca, do you understand?"

"Yes, Sir."

"But, Sir…" began Paget as he defended Craven's honour and refute that of Blakeney.

"No," Wellington cut the Lieutenant off abruptly.

Paget said nothing more.

"Now, the French are on the run, and I would pursue them whilst we still have strength. Will you join me, Major?"

"Of course."

"Then let's be on and at them!"

Both infantry and cavalry all around them were preparing to move to keep on the pursuit.

"Did we not do enough this past day?" Paget was following Craven as he rushed back for his horse and to gather all who would join him.

"Enough?" Craven snarled, "We will have done enough when every Frenchman is driven back into France, and then perhaps we shall do some more."

"You are angry, Sir, about General Le Marchant?"

"Him and many more," snapped Craven.

He reached their camp to find Ferreira and Matthys had them formed up and ready to move, with those on horseback already in the saddle. Craven, Paget, and Timmerman's horses having been made ready for them. Paget looked anxious as he rushed to Charlie and took Augustus from her. He carefully checked the saddle and tack, for he was most precious about it. Joze led Craven's horse out for him, and he climbed into the saddle to address them all. Fatigue seemed to have given way to something else, as if they had been reinvigorated.

"Why are they so eager?" Craven leant in over Matthys'

shoulder.

"Colonel Blakeney was a plague on them all, and you did something about it. You risked everything to do right by them and by those who have fallen."

Craven was stunned. It was the first time Matthys had celebrated his victory in a duel and been happy that he participated, and yet he knew something was different this time. They all did, none more so than Matthys. This time Craven did not fight a duel for himself and his own vanity, but for everyone else.

"Nothing more needs to be said, for you have said it in action."

Craven took a deep breath and felt a great weight lift from his shoulders. Matthys had always made him feel guilt for participating in duels and so many more awful things he had done, but this was different.

"I did the right thing?" he whispered.

"Yes, and they love you for it," smiled Matthys.

"Even if I had to kill a man?"

"That man was dead inside a long time ago. You only sealed his mouth shut."

Craven was stunned, as he rarely heard Matthys speak ill of any man, and so he now understood the severity of the situation and why the whole Regiment was behind him. Craven took a deep breath in relief as he put it behind him and thought of the path ahead.

"Yesterday we fought a great battle, the likes of which is certain to go down in the history books. Those who fought the hardest have earnt their rest, but the enemy is still out there, pressing on where they might regain their strength just as we have so many times. Lord Wellington gives pursuit and means to ride on after the enemy himself. Every one of you here has earnt that right to rest and let others go on in this duty, but I cannot, for I must see this fight through until the end. Will you come with me?"

They roared in agreement as they raised their hats, muskets, and swords into the air in support. Not one amongst them shied away as they formed up and quickly marched with a real spring in their step. They soon reached the assembled force with Wellington about to depart, leading the pursuit just as he said he would.

General Bock approached Craven as drew up in readiness to join the expedition.

"Sir," Craven saluted him.

"Major, Wellington means to pursue the enemy down all three roads which they have followed. Our duty is to take the Southern Road, the right flank. Le Marchant meant a great deal to us, as I knew he did to you. It would be an honour if you would ride with us just as you rode with him yesterday."

"A lowly Rifle officer riding with the heavies?" smiled Craven.

"We fight as one. You might not have been born to that uniform, but neither was I. My land was taken by Napoleon, and so I fight for Wellington, and my king, who is also your king," declared the Hanoverian.

He was an old soldier, close to sixty Craven imagined. He carried himself with a great nobility. A scar reached up under his cocked hat from what had to be a very old sword injury. But in spite of his accent, his uniform was little different to the one Le Marchant had worn, the same bright scarlet jacket with tails, white breeches, and tall black riding boots. Only the dark blue facings of his tunic were unique.

"What do you say? Will you ride with the heavies?"

Craven peered down at the sheathed light cavalry sabre fixed to his saddle. It was hardly appropriate for the heavy cavalry, and yet it was the same sword Le Marchant had brandished into battle.

"I would."

They were soon on their way. Ferreira led the dismounted force to join the infantry which pushed on as quickly as they could, knowing they would be many miles behind the cavalry as they gave chase. Yet thick clouds soon brought rain to dampen all of their spirits, though in this case it was a welcome reprieve from the burning hot fields of the dry battlefield the day before. The mounted element rode on with the heavies in what felt more like a hunt than a march to battle, and yet they were all aware that if the retreating army were to rally and stand against them, it would be no light jolly as it was being treated.

Soon enough they stumbled across masses of baggage that had been dumped by the retreating French forces. Carts had been abandoned and many supplies were strewn about the roads. Many a French soldier who could not keep up through injury or fatigue had been left behind. They were all the scenes of a defeated army fleeing in panic. For they were leaving behind valuable soldiers and resources which they could not afford to lose.

Paget watched many of the wounded with suspicion as they rode on by, as if expecting some sort of ambush.

"They are no threat to us now," insisted Craven.

"I am afraid I am not so sure, Sir. How many times have

we waited in ambush for the French?"

"Because we planned for it far into the wilderness. The whole British army advances along these roads now, and they know it."

Paget wasn't satisfied and continued to keep a keen eye on the French soldiers as they passed by. Some had thrown their muskets down. Others used them as crutches, and some rested with them about their bodies as if ready to use them, but mostly they just looked entirely exhausted. Unable to move or even think about their next action.

"Did you really aim at the middle of Blakeney, Sir?" Paget finally asked as he tried to take his worried mind off of what troubled it, only to step from the frying pan into the fire.

"Why does that surprise you so?"

"I just cannot understand why a man so precise with the blade would do such a thing."

"It was the best chance I had of making the shot. Anything else was too much of a gamble. I might be a terrible gambler, but I gamble with money. I do not gamble with my life, nor the lives of those I command."

Paget was remarkably relieved to hear it.

"I thought you…I thought you had other reasons, Sir."

"Did you think I wanted to die at the hands of Colonel Blakeney?"

"I don't know, Sir, but I cannot fathom why you would accept a duel with pistols. What a tragedy it would be for one of the greatest swordsmen of our generation to die at the hands of a pistol in a duel?"

"I wouldn't choose it, but I had to see it done. Blakeney endangered us all, and there are enough dangers in this land which we face already."

"I feel a great weight is lifted, then, Sir. We mourn what we have lost, but we must also celebrate what we have gained. A great victory in Spain. A victory so many said could not be done. Thinking of General Le Marchant, it was not so long ago that the officers under his command and many generals believed the war would soon end, not because of our victory, but because we would abandon Spain, and Portugal, too."

"And yet here we are. If only we could see the look on Napoleon's face when he receives this news," smiled Craven.

"Yes, Sir, only two days ago I saw local people abandoning their homes and cursing the name of Wellington. That we would abandon them without a fight, and now we are triumphant. Not a shallow victory like Talavera. I know it is spoken of so fondly, and it was a victory no doubt, but not like this. This was the test we had all been waiting for."

On they marched for several miles. The tracks were well worn where masses of French troops had fled. The road was becoming quite rough and rocky, but on they pressed. Finally, many miles on they caught a glimpse of the rear guard of the French army taking refuge in a French village ahead. Bock drew them to a halt, but he did not even lift a glass to look for himself, unlike Craven, Paget, and several of Bock's squadron commanders.

The village was full, with French infantry drawing water from the wells after an exhausting night and forced march.

"What do you see?" Bock asked.

"Infantry throughout the town and cavalry between us and them." Craven then offered his glass to Bock.

"It would do no good, I cannot see that far," he boldly

claimed.

Craven was stunned as he looked to Paget to find a similar expression, but the cavalrymen around them showed no surprise at all as the squadron commanders got on with their work. Craven took out his map to get a better idea of what they were looking at.

"That is the village of Garcia Hernandez. The road through it goes Northeast. Wellington gave pursuit across all three roads, but here I think we have found the rear guard. The infantry there in the village look fresh, like they did not fight a battle yesterday. The last remnants that recovered in good order."

"Which cannot be said for their cavalry," declared Paget as he looked at the sorry state that the French Chasseurs were in.

"Look, Sir," said Paget.

The guns of some French horse artillery were being unlimbered well into the distance and readied to fire. The village itself sprang alive as the infantry there hurried to form up outside the town and continue their march, not looking as though they wanted to do battle. On the British marched as they closed in. The village was emptied well before Wellington's force got into distance, of which most were glad. Few would want a gruelling skirmish through the narrow streets and houses of the village. It felt good to for once be the one pursuing the rear guard and not part of it, as Craven and his comrades had been so many times in the past years.

"Do we force an engagement, Sir?" Paget asked.

Craven looked over to Wellington who was looking on upon the village from the head of the light cavalry he had led after the enemy.

"I don't think we came after them merely to speed their withdrawal," replied Craven.

"It could be a dangerous thing to force battle on a wounded animal. They might flee, or they might fight like hell," said Matthys.

The first French cannon fired, and it was as though it were a starting pistol as Wellington urged on the British light cavalry. They charged on to sweep away the French cavalry force defending the Western edge of Garcia Hernandez. A rider came galloping up to Bock.

"Lord Wellington requests that you turn the flank of the cavalry, Sir!" cried the man.

"And so we will!" Bock roared.

The messenger vanished but Bock looked to Craven for help.

"Where are they?"

"Who, Sir?"

"The bloody French, the French cavalry!"

Craven was stunned as he realised just how poor the General's vision really was, as he could not make out the mass of Chasseurs ahead of them.

"There, sir," Craven pointed.

"Come on, then!"

They were in motion in no time at all as the orders were passed on to squadron leaders. They advanced just as quickly, as they had managed to get into formation after travelling across the narrow and stony roads that had led them there. They all knew what they were getting themselves into. Matthys was right. To force an engagement was dangerous, especially as the British infantry lagged so far behind, including Ferreira and the rest of the Salford Rifles. All Wellington had at his disposal was cavalry, and cavalry alone could not win a pitched battle if it came to it. That was the doctrine they all well understood.

"What if the infantry turns to fight, Sir?"

"Then we will be in a spot of bother!" Craven smiled back at Paget.

It did not put off the cavalry who rode forward with such great enthusiasm that one might think they were immortal, for the loss of Gaspard Le Marchant weighed heavily on them all. He meant a great deal to the light and heavy cavalry alike. He had served a great many years with both across many regiments, and his involvement in founding the military academy meant he had endeared himself to many a young cavalry officer. The first students of which were experiencing war for the first time in the same conflict their mentor had fought beside them in and died for.

Craven could see it on their faces. They felt no fatigue from the battle the day before. No fear for facing the enemy once more. They rode with purpose, and nothing was going to stop them. Garcia Hernandez looked to be nothing more than a small skirmish, but the cavalry thundered on as if they rode to the centre of the whole French army, and they would not be stopped. The memory of Le Marchant rode on beside them.

The British light cavalry reached the enemy first, but the exhausted and bedraggled French cavalry did not look interested in standing to fight against such a relentless force, and they buckled without a fight. Hundreds of French Chasseurs fled the scene, riding off in complete confusion before a shot was fired or sabres clashed. They vanished in a cloud of dust, the British light cavalry pursuing them relentlessly. Bock's heavy cavalry were not far behind, but it seemed like the skirmish would peter out into a dislodgement and short chase than any sort of battle.

And yet a volley of musket fire rippled out at their flank, and a number of the German cavalry were knocked from their saddles. They looked to their flank to behold a vast body of French infantry, more than two thousand of them concealed by the light cavalry and the undulations of the ground. The nearest battalions were formed in square, one of which had given they volley and now hurried to reload. It was a cavalryman's nightmare. For cavalry could not break a well-maintained square without cannon or infantry, just like Le Marchant's great success against a crumbling square the day before that had been savaged by volleys of the British infantry.

It seemed an impossible situation as the cavalry formation galloped on in parallel with the French squares. They could receive more fire, or they could withdraw. Those were the only choices which made any sense. For the morning light glistened upon the raindrops clinging to thousands of French bayonets that seemed impregnable. The German cavalry was in complete disorder, having expected to be charging down the bedraggled French cavalry that was easy pickings for them, only to be struck in their flank by a most unwelcome volley and a terrifying sight.

"By God!" Bock cried as he saw the French squares. For he could see them in spite of his dreadful sight, which was hardly surprising. How could anyone miss several thousand French soldiers firing and bearing their bayonets at you? For a moment the leading German cavalry regiment was in complete confusion, but cries rang out from the squadron leaders as they took charge and rallied the other squadrons before Bock could think of planning anything. An excited Captain cried out for his squadron to do the unthinkable. He led them forward as they wheeled and made a charge directly for the square.

It seemed like suicide, and yet the Germans charged as though they had God on their side, or at least Le Marchant watching over them from up high. Few could believe what they were seeing, as Craven looked back to where Wellington had ordered the attack. He watched on with disbelief, knowing that the events were beyond his control. As the German heavy cavalry squadron reached within eighty yards of the square, a volley rang out and downed several more of the one hundred and forty cavalrymen.

It was a tiny force, and yet they charged as though they were ten times their number, as if they would not be turned away, no matter what. At twenty yards another volley erupted from the square to far worse and destructive effect. Many of the Germans and their horses were down, but one of the horses at the front collapsed into a tumble and rolled, crashing in through the ranks of the square. The wounded animal kicked out in all directions from its back, knocking over a dozen French infantry and causing them to scatter. It created a path into the square. The rest of the German cavalry looked upon the opening with glee as if Moses himself had parted the way, and they stormed on through it to exploit the opening before the enemy could recover.

It was a most amazing sight to behold. The rest of the small battlefield seemed to freeze, and all watched in bewilderment as the Heavy Dragoons of the King's German Legion rang amok inside the square. Their horses crashed into the infantrymen, and their great big straight swords hammered down upon them, splitting skulls left and right. The square collapsed completely for the cavalry were all amongst them. Some tried to run, but most threw down their weapons in surrender.

Wellington stood up in his saddle and waved his hat about in the air frenetically as he could hardly believe what he had seen. The KGL had achieved what many said was impossible, and they had now killed or captured five times their own number in one short and brisk charge. Bock could not see far, but he understood the events as it was unmistakeable as cheers rang out all around him.

"Onwards, finish them!" he cried out.

Few could hear his orders, but they did not need to, as the momentum was well in the favour of the German cavalry. Many of the French soldiers fled for the protection of the hills as at their backs was a squadron of the KGL. The French infantry were shaken by the unthinkable and devastating loss of the first square, but they still turned and gave several harrowing volleys as the heavy cavalry approached them. But it did no good. The Germans rushed in amongst them and began to sabre a great many as they had done on the flat ground.

It was chaos everywhere you looked. The seemingly strong French positions collapsed all around, and the cavalry scattered them in every direction. A mass of the KGL from three different squadrons and the Salford Rifles advanced on a square that had formed on the skyline, where one French battalion was being reinforced by all who had fled the dragoons. It was amassing the strongest position of all. The Chasseurs who had fled earlier now formed on their flank in readiness to launch a counter charge, but this did not deter the KGL and Salford

Rifles, who galloped uphill for three hundred yards.

It was a charge that any experienced cavalryman would consider insane, reckless, or suicidal even. For they exhausted their mounts and rushed upon a well-prepared square assembled with a great many veteran troops. Nothing was in the favour of the charging cavalry. Not speed on the long incline, not numbers, not firepower, nor fresh mounts, nor any support. And the French Chasseurs were almost licking their lips with glee as they waited for their chance for revenge. There was no reason to think the charge of the heavy dragoons could succeed, except for the unwavering minds and hearts of all who made the charge.

Musket fire erupted, and several dragoons went down, but the enemy seemed to quake in fear as the heavy cavalry thundered towards them. With the image of the first French square crumbling still fresh in their minds it was as if nothing would stop them, as they swept forward like a crashing wave. The square became disordered just a little as the mix of different battalions and stragglers struggled to maintain discipline in the face of such a determined and relentless assault. They were still in square, but the weakness of the formation was enough, and nothing was going to stop the heavies as they thundered into the square.

Craven and his small band of mounted Rifles rode in beside them, hacking and slashing all about, just as the troopers of the King's German Legion did. Birback whirled about and smashed down with his sabre like a madman. For a moment they were all caught up in the frenzy, and in that moment, they were all fighting for their lives, as if the infantry did not break quickly, they were in for a bloody melee.

Timmerman looked as animated as the German heavies as he drove his horse into a body of infantry and began hammering down upon them. One officer lifted a pistol to fire at him, but Timmerman got up in his stirrups and brought his sabre down with such power that the hand wielding the pistol was cleaved away before it could pull the trigger. The officer cried out as he cradled his bloody stump and ran from the crumbling square. The terror was beginning to set in. Those in the square had felt safe within it against cavalry alone, and yet the devils they battled seemed to have no care for the rules of nature as they blasted through their defences as if they were nothing.

Vicenta ran on through but then struggled to find another target, as cavalrymen all around her were crashing on through the French position, hammering away in all directions. Charlie pushed on past Paget to engage one who was coming for the Lieutenant. She cut his bayonet away and hacked down into the Frenchman's shoulder, causing him to drop his weapon and flee as quickly as he could. Another Frenchman thrust at her and missed her body. The bayonet passed through the gap between her fingers and the war iron of her sabre. The blade scraped her fingers bloody, but it stuck there. She took hold of the muzzle, locking it in place before pulling her sabre clear of the bayonet. She held the blade up to strike the young man down but froze for a moment as she saw the fear in his eyes. It was a fear she had seen before in the people she loved. She could not go through with her strike, and the man let go of the musket, throwing up his hands in surrender.

Paget had watched it unfold and was captivated. It was the first time he had seen her rein in her anger and hatred of the enemy in battle. It was the first time he had seen her show mercy. A cheer rang out from the cavalrymen around them, and they looked about to see the square was fractured. And some men began to run, but many threw down their muskets and would fight no more. The French Chasseurs who had waited for their moment to shine fled with their tails between their legs, not daring to make a charge at what seemed like an unbeatable foe.

It was clear to see why when they looked back at the devastation across the battlefield. They had been significantly outnumbered when the battle began, and the surprise of finding a vast force of French infantry formed and ready to repel cavalry seemed like a trap they could not escape, and yet they had turned the tables and won the most unlikely of victories. Cheers rang out from them all as they celebrated with immense relief.

Bock came to a halt beside Craven as a number of his dragoons ran on after the enemy, attempting to rush yet another square as many of the French soldiers fled behind it. It was a step too far, and yet the cavalrymen were caught up in the excitement and could not help themselves. Nobody could blame them for it after the incredible achievements of this day. Although they were met with more resistance, and many were shot down. The rest soon swerved away to disengage from battle. The engagement was over, for the British cavalry were spent, but the damage to the French army was beyond belief. Nearly fifteen hundred prisoners were led away and several hundred lay dead on the field, and yet there were so few German casualties from the units that had inflicted the damage.

It was without doubt one of the most spectacular charges any of them had ever seen or heard of, and a decisive victory. It only served to amplify the victory at Salamanca and seal the fate of Marmont's so-called Army of Portugal, who were now on the run deep into Spain.

The rain was easing, and the final wafts of powder smoke was disseminating. It was the blades of swords that had been triumphant that day. Brute force tactics and the cleaving arms of the cavalry had won the day. The enemy rear guard continued their withdrawal, and they were safe for now, but at a terrible loss that day. The cavalry atop the hill cried out in triumph, and a great mass of the French infantry were led away as prisoners. Masses of their muskets had been laid down upon the field where they had formed squares, and the weapons remained in much of the same formation, revealing just how many had surrendered.

"Sir?" Paget asked as he panted heavily from the exertion of a frenetic combat.

"Yes?" Craven answered him.

"Sir, General Le Marchant said he would make a cavalryman of you, and he was right."

Craven looked down at the light cavalry sabre he had used in the charge. He remembered the moment Le Marchant had given it to him like it was yesterday. It was not the sort of sword he favoured nor would ever have purchased for himself, or not since being a young man. For before he knew much about fencing, he had always admired a great big hacking blade, and yet years of practice had made him take a different path. And yet here he was with such a sword in hand, but not only was he carrying it, he was using the weapon to fearsome and triumphant success. The same sword he had used to end Mizon, who was a thorn in their side throughout.

"I didn't think I'd ever care about the life of a general," he smiled.

"He was a swordsman and a brother in arms, like the rest of us," replied Paget solemnly.

"Yes, he was."

"And the purse of money the General gave you, Sir?"

"I acquired a great sword just as I promised him, and my oath is fulfilled. But I also made another promise. The purse will go to whoever ends Bouchard, and I will keep to my word. He is not a man to toy with. I will not show compassion towards that bastard again, nor let my own pride get in the way of what must be done. We will find him, just like we found Mizon."

Bock rode up beside them to watch the enemy continue their flight, though Craven wondered how much of it he could really see.

"The name Salamanca might be remembered forever, but what you did here will also," declared Craven.

"What we did, Major, for we did not do it alone."

Craven shrugged as it felt like they were merely along for the ride. They had done little, and yet it felt incredible to be a part of making history.

"Three squares broken by cavalry alone. I never thought I would see the day," replied Craven.

"It is a day of firsts," smiled Paget.

He looked to Charlie, proud that she had managed to stay her hand in the heat of battle, just as he had the day before at Salamanca. She had ridiculed him for it then, but now it was her turn to do the same, and she was starting to let go off her bloodlust. Paget was beaming. The cavalry charge with the heavies was a dream come true, and for it to be such an overwhelming success against all odds only amplified it to new heights. Finally, they had a moment to catch a breath and realise what had been achieved over the past two days. For weeks and months, they had chased and been chased by Marmont's army. For so long it seemed as though nothing would be achieved, and now the scales had tipped entirely in their favour. Craven noticed he was deep in thought and had to enquire the reasons for it.

"What is it?"

"This is what we needed, isn't it, Sir? This is the victory Sir Arthur was chasing?"

"It is, and it will send shockwaves throughout all of Europe, all the way back to France and England," smiled Craven.

"You think Napoleon will hear of this, Sir?" Paget asked excitedly that his exploits might be brought to the Emperor's attention.

"Of course, and he will surely be furious."

Timmerman galloped up beside them with a massive smile on his face as if he was enjoying every second of it.

"I didn't think for a moment you would really ride with us, not at Salamanca and not here today," declared Craven.

"Is this what it is like to live the life of Major James Craven?"

Craven shrugged, for it was not the norm, and yet it was hard to deny that it was what his life had become.

"You came here to make your fortune but let me tell you now. You will be a rich man when you return to England, for I will make sure you have the opportunities to make it so."

Craven shrugged once more.

"That is not what you wanted? I am surprised."

"It was. It was what I desired more than anything not so

very long ago."

"And now?"

"Now this feels more like home than England did, and so I want victory."

Timmerman laughed.

"Has the rogue finally become a soldier?"

"One could say the same about you, I should think."

"Yes, I suppose you could." Timmerman paused in reflection to think about it and realised how far they had both come from their brawling and selfish days.

"Will it make a difference what we did here?" Paget asked.

"Most certainly, my lad!" Wellington cried as he rode up to join them and marvel at the French rear guard, which now fled having been so badly mauled.

"Then it was all worth it," muttered Paget to himself.

"Nothing is worth the lives we have lost these past days and these past years, but it must be done. And if it must be done, then we will see it done well," insisted Wellington.

"Yes, Sir," agreed Paget.

Wellington marvelled at Craven and Timmerman sitting side by side in the saddle and making no attempt to kill one another.

"I pity the French whilst you two fight side by side and not against one another," declared Wellington.

"It is a match made in hell," replied Paget.

Wellington looked stunned, wondering if the Lieutenant meant it as an insult, and yet both men took it in good spirits as they laughed together. Watching the enemy flee into the distance brought a great joy and relief to them all, as until only a few days before it seemed like an unreachable task. Wellington took a

deep breath and let out a long gasp as though a huge weight had been lifted from his shoulders. Wellington and his army had proven that they could beat the French, not just in a defensive battle, but going forward. Madrid was now within their grasp.
"Gentlemen, the battle for Portugal is finally over, and the battle for Spain has now begun!"

THE END

Printed in Great Britain
by Amazon